This page is intentionaly left blank.

© 2020 Carnival of Glee Creations

William Allen Pepper

Hell's Cereal: Very Short Stories Fortified With Essential Syllables

All rights reserved. The stories contained herein originally appeared in whole or in part on the "Atari Bytes" podcast, copyright 2016-2020. No part of this publication may be reproduced, stored in a retrieval system or transmited in any form or by any means, electronic, mechanical, photocopying, recording or otherwise without the prior permision of the publisher or in accordance with the provisions of the Copyright, Designs and Patents Act 1988 or under the terms of any licence permitting limited copying issued by the Copyright Licensing Angency.. In a promotional capacity, brief quotations may be used so long as the author and original source are properly credited.

This book is published in the United States of America by Carnival of Glee Creations. This book is a work of fiction. The characters, events, dialogue, and plots are products of the author's imagination. Any similarities to actual persons or events, living or dead, is purely coincidental. No infringement of existing copyright is intended.

Published by: Carnival of Glee Creations

Text and Cover Design by: Wiliam Allen Pepper

A CIP record for this book is available from the Library of Congress Cataloging-in-Publication Data

Paperback ISBN: 978-0-9818647-5-4

E-Book ISBN: 978-0-9818647-6-1

Distributed by: Carnival of Glee Creations

William Allen Pepper

HELL'S CEREAL

VERY SHORT STORIES FORTIFIED WITH ESSENTIAL SYLLABLES

Carnival of Glee Creations

Dedicated to Henry, my frequent ATARI BYTES cohost, and Sophie, who rolls her eyes a lot.

Also by WILLIAM ALLEN PEPPER:

Misery Banana: Very Short Stories Inspired by Old Games and Odd Thoughts

In the St. Nick of TIme (as William Pepper)

HELL'S CEREAL

VERY SHORT STORIES FORTIFIED WITH
ESSENTIAL SYLLABLES

WILLIAM ALLEN PEPPER

BY WAY OF AN INTRODUCTION. SORT OF.

The author chews a spoonful of sugary delight, lost in anticipation of the secret toy surprise at the bottom of the cereal box. Suddenly, he realizes he's not alone. Dabbing a dribble of milk off his chin, he gestures with the spoon. "Oh, hi," he says. "Welcome."

In the very first episode of the ATARI BYTES podcast, I talked about the iconic game "Yar's Revenge". In many ways, the game is emblematic of what video games were. Are. Probably always will be.

Wait! Don't close this book! Never heard of "Yar's Revenge"? Or Atari? Or the podcast? Don't worry. All this is prelude; a look inside my head to see what spawned the stories in this book. Once completed, the stories are their own abomination; minimally, at best, tied to the games featured in the episodes of the show. Just follow me for a few more paragraphs.

"Yar's Revenge" takes place in the cold darkness of space. Your "Yar" is on the left of the neutral zone and an alien-autopsy-looking spaceman is on the right. Honestly, he looks like the triangle-headed, huge-eyed alien you see on every alien autopsy show.

You're the aggressor, really, not the avenger. You might as well be the Godfather - space Corleone, if you will – what with the kiss of death you lay on the alien and all

There's a spaceman head in the game that doesn't really do anything. And a floating Pez candy bugging you, but that's about it.

You blast down the space face's force field, kiss the alien, then blast his butt with a photon torpedo or something. Sometimes the autopsy alien turns into a blood red spiral of death and tries to annihilate you... but who hasn't done that?

The photon torpedo homes in on your position. If you don't move, you get blasted. Just you, moving around the screen, trying to stay alive. Describes pretty much any Atari game ever. And life too.

This is actually kind of a creepy, lonely game. Like one of those stories where the hero and the enemy are trapped together and have to decide whether to kill each other or find peace. Like Picard and the Tamarian captain in the Star Trek: The Next Generation episode "Darmok" or that Lou Gossett/Dennis Quaid movie Enemy Mine.

In those stories, the enemies become allies. In this game from decades ago, at least one of you dies. Both of you, really, because once you turn the game console off, it's all over. Everyone in that game world, so recently brought to vibrant life, ceases to be once again.

Countless worlds spread out before you in video games. Beneath every Yar, every Mario, every "Burger Time" chef and gorilla with a paint roller (looking at you, "Amidar"), there's inspiration for a wide range of stories; settings, names, plots off of which a story can spiral like that autopsy alien spiral of death. Sometimes for me - okay most of the time - the story spiral lands somewhere completely different. Could be another planet, could be this planet. Yesterday, today, tomorrow. Alone or in a huge crowd. Fantasy, sci-fi, family or workplace drama, spy adventure, flat out comedy, even occasionally bad poetry. Often as not, I build a whole story off just the title of a game without knowing anything about the game itself.

Every week, I pick a new game and write a new short story from scratch. The games are writing prompts for me, not required playing for you; though I would totally recommend you play. These games are excellent.

Thus, ATARI BYTES was born. And, by extension, this book. You're welcome! Now, if you'll excuse me, I need to go grab that toy out of the cereal box before my kids get it.

SPEAKEASY, BUT GET THIS DAMN MONKEY OFF MY BACK

Niles's toothache wouldn't have bothered him near as much if the flapper riding in the passenger seat of his roaring Bugatti 35 racer would shut up.

His passenger's bracelets clacked together as her hands waved. "This auto is the bee's knees," she shouted.

"Leave me alone," Niles shouted.

"Rhatz," with a prominent "h" and a "z", she pouted playfully, still smiling.

But then, she was gone.

The Bugatti barreled down the road. Niles had to get there. He didn't know where "there" was exactly - wherever it was, he would be the first to arrive.

Sweat - and tears maybe - blurred his vision. He wiped an already moist sleeve across his face just in time to swerve the Bugatti away from smearing the flapper who now stood in the middle of the road. Her gams woulda been no better than kindling if Niles wasn't such a good driver.

"I'm good, I'm good," he told himself.

The flapper was gone again. Only the road remained. Just Niles and his road. Like always. The road to somewhere. And nowhere.

The road bubbled and curved. Rippling like a pond. Niles wasn't just driving a car. He was commanding a mighty vessel.

But then his tooth pain roared forth. Niles whimpered.

"Hey, spiffy," the flapper said, again in the seat next to him. "Let's you and me find a gin mill. A little hooch'll fix up that kisser of yours."

"Scram, would ya?" Niles said. "I know what I need."

"Yeah, a fine ol' whoopee if you ask me," the flapper said.

"I said 'scram,'" Niles yelled, reaching across the woman to open the passenger side door.

Laughing as she rolled out, the flapper called, "Don't be such a bluenose, bub." She disappeared before she hit the ground.

Niles gripped the wheel as both lifeline and enemy. His tooth throbbed. He needed a dentist. A special dentist. One who had just the right touch.

Lights appeared up ahead. A car was approaching. The Bugatti's tires crunched through the gravel on the shoulder of the road. Niles wanted to turn and flee. He knew what that car was. Crashin' Clyde - that's what Niles called it - had pursued Niles for years. Niles couldn't shake him.

Clyde approached, head on. Never slowing. In the game of chicken, Niles blinked first and swerved. Niles always blinked. He hated himself for it, but always got back out on the road.

Even with Clyde behind him, the road had gotten longer somehow. Niles's tooth seemed to be barking orders now.

A large, rabid canine. Snarling. Drooling. Running alongside the Bugatti. Crashin' Clyde held the leash, gave a salute with his other hand. Niles tried to swerve away, but Clyde was persistent.

Niles gunned it. Clyde kept apace.

The Bugatti rolled to a stop in front of the office of Dr. Wilson Winston, DDS. Niles leapt frantically from the car, stumbled inside in a spray of sweat and desperation.

Dr. Winston sat with his feet up on the desk, reading a newspaper.

"Doc, you gotta hook me up," Niles said. "My tooth is killing me."

Winston barely looked up from the box scores. "You were just here yesterday."

"Yeah, weird huh?" Niles said.

"Is it your left molar?"

"That's the one."

"I pulled that last week," Winston said.

"Oh," Niles said. "I thought you meant MY left, your right."

"I did," Dr. Winston said, still not looking up.

"Uh..."

"You're wasting your time, Niles," Dr. Winston said, neatly folding the paper and placing it on the desk before him. "Scientists have figured out the addictive properties of cocaine outweigh its usefulness as an anesthetic. It's pretty heavily regulated now." Winston shrugged.

Niles's pounding heart sent the blood rushing through his ears, so he wasn't sure he heard right. "So...no coke then?"

Winston shook his head. "Well, my brother's a bootlegger so I've got a bottle of bathtub gin and some rusty pliers..." He laughed. Niles did not.

Niles beat it out of the dentist's office.

"Hold on, Niles," Dr. Winston called after him. "I was kidding. Let me help."

The Bugatti left rubber as Niles sped off to he knew not where. But he could still hear Crashin' Clyde laughing over his shoulder...

This story was inspired by ATARI BYTES episode 157: DODGE 'EM, though I can't remember anything other than cars in that game that would explain this. See what you're in for?

THE FUTURE, MADE TO ORDER

December 26 is a day for reflection at the North Pole. As the elves scramble to winterize the sleigh, ice down the reindeers' joints and store all the empty toy bags, Nick gives Mrs. Claus his candy cane, then takes a long winter nap. But time works differently at the pole, so he's up in time for a sugary brunch.

With his appetites sated, Nick then convenes a meeting of his senior elf staff to do a postmortem on the Christmas gift distribution. This administrative stuff is boring and makes Nick crabby. That does not bode well for head elf Sam.

Sam had been an elf at the pole for centuries. He became Head of Wrapping and Distribution around the time America became a country. Under his tenure, present wrapping became more efficient- not every package needs a bow, save scraps left from wrapping large boxes to wrap small ones, don't go nuts with the tape. Stuff like that. Plus, distribution of outgoing gifts to Santa's bags was quicker so he got the presents down the chimneys faster.

Sam had been considering asking for a raise. Another gingerbread per hour. It didn't seem unreasonable.

And so, Sam was perplexed when Santa asked to meet with him alone. Santa was a people person. He liked a group dynamic. One-on-one wasn't a good arrangement for Santa. Past Santas had secretly infiltrated the mall Santa world. Not Nick. He couldn't handle it. It got creepy and weird. There are a couple malls in the Detroit area he can't go to anymore. So for him to ask to meet alone with Sam… well, that couldn't be good.

Sam thought this year was pretty flawless. Yeah, a couple kids in Holland were confused when they got the surfboards meant for kids in the Florida Keys who instead got wooden shoes. That sort of thing is bound to happen in a network as huge as the pole. And there was that family at the parsonage in Alberta whose gifts were wrapped in pornographic gift wrap, but that was a system hack by the bitter, outgoing Tooth Fairy and not Sam's fault.

"Have a seat, Sam," Nick said, voice and eye-twinkle both muted. His coat was off. One fire-engine red suspender strap was over his beefy shoulder, the other hung limp at his waste. Was that a cocoa stain on his shirt? This early in the day?

Sam flopped down in a marshmallow-shaped chair. He was nervous, wanted to fill the space with his own voice as he feared what Santa's booming voice might bring. "I've got some ideas for after the post-Christmas break," Sam said in a rush. "If we start now, I think we can overhaul the whole world distribution system by next Christmas. Tough, but doable. I'm thinking an alphabetical system."

"Sounds good," Santa said, but his words didn't match his tone. He clearly wasn't listening. "But...well, you see.."

"And we have new data on the most pleasing wrapping paper colors.." Sam started to say, in rapid-fire. Santa raised his hand.

"Sam, wait. I have to tell you something," Nick said. "North Pole Industries...Well, the other holiday icons are withholding a larger percentage of our funding. Politics, you know…" The disturbingly not so jolly elf paused to gather himself. "Ho ho ho-boy this is hard."

"We've had cuts before," Sam said. "We always find room in the budget." In one particularly brutal year, reindeer hoof polishing and long-distance to the Real World had been cut to save money. The Pole was about giving; it was getting harder to justify their existence on a spreadsheet when there was only money going out and none coming in. Even magical accounting couldn't fix that forever. "We'll get through this, Santa," Sam concluded. "All of us."

"Not this time," St. Nick said. "Cutbacks have to be made…"

"Well, it's not like we can leave a bill under the tree for services rendered," Sam said, hearing himself almost shout.

The rest of the conversation was a blur of mutual reassurances and bland hot chocolate.

Sam cleaned out his locker and Charlie-Brown-walked from Santa's workshop, pockets full of severance candy canes and broken heart empty. Whatever would he do now?

***

That was seven years ago. A blip in the long life of an elf. Usually…

"I said, 'hold the onion,'" the man with the tiny face and huge glasses said. His chin quivered a bit from nerves or really misplaced rage.

"Oh," Sam said, slump-shouldered. "Sorry." He clearly was not so much sorry as annoyed at having to do this over again.

Sam stomped back to the assembly room. Burger after burger rolled by. The food dispenser fired in rapid succession and endless combinations. Just cheese. Cheese, lettuce, tomato. Onion, lettuce, tomato. Cheese and onion. Lettuce and onion. Cheese and tomato. Just lettuce. There was no end to it.

Sam looked around. Where the hell were the other workers? There weren't any. That's where they were. It was all machines. Just the machines and him. The machines worked because that's what they do. Sam worked because minimum wage was...well, minimal...but it was a wage. When he was at the Pole, a few candy canes per week got you a pretty nice apartment overlooking Yuletide Lane. But in the real world, you needed a little cash to put a roof over your head. Never mind chimney maintenance, which might seem like an extravagance for someone so poor, but he had to be ready for Christmas night. Didn't he?

He chuckled darkly; looked around for someone to chuckle with. There was no one, of course. Just the whir of the food dispenser depositing unused tomatoes on the floor at his feet like so many Christmas ornaments waiting to be put into service lifting holiday spirits.

Sam missed the elves. He missed running the wrapping division at the pole. Now he was just a grunt, taking orders from a faceless assistant manager. He did have a face, of course, and a name, probably. Tommy. Or maybe Tony. Wait. No. It was Marie.

It wasn't even about being in charge. Sam missed being with the elves; working together toward a common purpose of making people happy.

Now he assembled and packaged burgers for whiny kids and dude bros and harried parents, all of whom would forget his efforts before they crapped out the fruits of his labor.

An errant bun beaned Sam in the head, snapping him out of his funk. He was worth more than the prevailing wage. He had more to offer than greasy, grey globs of saturated fat.

Sam tossed his chef coat into a pile of lettuce, then quickly retrieved it. He had paid for that. The assistant manager had asked him to wear a "The Grille" t-shirt. (The "e" at the end is for "excellence".) Sam refused because the franchise mascot was supposed to be a zebra - don't know why - but it really just looked like Vixen in his Halloween costume. Thinking of the reindeer made Sam sad.

The assistant manager - now Sam thought maybe the manager's name was Brenda - protested for a few days, but the burgers were coming out hotter than ever so the customers' fries didn't get cold waiting. So now Sam could wear whatever he wanted.

Well, mostly. He missed the curled shoes with the happy little bells. And the hats. The way the snow glistened in the sunset as he walked home on Yuletide Lane. Christmas production would be ramping up right about now. He remembered the intense joy in the air at the pole this time of year. He missed that too, probably most of all. Oh, hell, he missed his old life. All of it.

So, he was going to take it back.

Sam stomped toward the restaurant back door. He was just about out when the assistant manager - let's say Reynaldo - burst in from the condiment room. "Sam," he said. "We need you! A bus is coming. Huge order. Burgers are backlogged. The tabs on those little square boxes never line up." The weary assistant manager's breath came out in ragged spurts.

"Look…Carl?…I –" Sam started to say.

"Sam," the manager interrupted. "We need you."

Sam hung his head. This was his chance. He should go right now.

"Sam," Possibly Sven said. "Hurry. The lids! Think of the lids."

Sam opened the door to the alley, then slammed it shut.

But he was still inside.

Sam was a professional first; a quitter never.

His employer needed him.

"Oliver," Sam said to the assistant manager. "Forget the boxes for the singles. There's no time. I'll need fifty yards of the waxed wrapping for the single burgers. Forty burger boxes for the doubles."

Assistant Manager Ernestine looked panicked.

"I can walk you through it," Sam said. "Move."

Not since the invention of origami has so much paper flown in such intricate patterns. Before this day, no fast food customer knew their double mushroom and Swiss needed to be wrapped in waxed paper shaped like the Eiffel Tower. But once the burger arrived on those colored plastic trays in such splendor, the customers couldn't live without these works of art.

Once they got ahead of the orders a bit, the assistant manager, Kamala, sent Sam out to the counter to take payment from the bus driver for the huge order.

"Fine..." Sam said, dying a little bit more inside.

Real world money seemed so…not fun. At the Pole, they traded in candy canes and cookies. Here, they just used bits of paper or metal; or some sort of magic plastic cards.

But Sam was a team player, so to the register he went.

Eyes downcast because the area behind the counter tended to be disturbingly sticky and he didn't want to fall, he stepped to the cash register and said, "Welcome to The Grille. We hope you're having a grill-celent day."

"Ho ho holy -sh-," the big man on the other side of the counter said.

Sam's eyes shot up and met the twinkly orbs and rosy cheeks of St. Nick himself. A partridge-sized lump formed in Sam's throat and he barely croaked out, "H-h hello-Nick."

"Sam, my dear boy," Santa said. "I'm so glad to have found you here."

"Because you've come to hire me back!" Sam blurted out. So much for playing it cool.

Santa chortled. "Oh, my Sam," he said. "No, no. The elves and I are just hungry. I know I can rely on you to get my onion rings extra crispy."

"Oh," Sam said. "Well, we aim to please." Assistant manager Kaiser Wilhelm shoveled bags full of food forward.

"He's the best," the assistant manager beamed.

"That's my boy," Santa said. "Did you remember the tartar sauce for the fish sandwiches?"

"Of course," Sam said, plastic smile rivaling the Barbie doll knock-offs they cranked out at the Pole. In truth, The Grille hadn't stocked tartar sauce for years. The packets in Santa's bag were from a dusty, unmarked box, on site since sometime after the restaurant first opened. Extreme revenge might be unhealthy, but little revenges never hurt anyone.

"Take care, Sam," Nick said, as he turned to leave.

"You too, Santa."

Santa left, getting half way back to the pole before finding out Sam also put holes in all the drink straws.

Fa la la la la la la la LA

Inspired by ATARI BYTES episode 158: PRESSURE COOKER, though I'm not exactly sure how. Also, I still love you, Kris Kringle!

WALL-EYED

The rain drops spattering on the office window provided a convenient distraction from Dr. Karpala's question.

"Roger," Dr. Karpala said. "Did you hear me?"

Roger Lipton, archaeologist, wished he could entomb himself in the cushions of his psychiatrist's couch, unsightly orange plaid notwithstanding.

"I said," Dr. Karpala pressed, "Do you think you put up walls between yourself and others?"

Lipton squirmed and chuckled a little, stroking his auburn, gray flecked beard. "I'm an archaeologist. Mostly I excavate where walls used to be."

"You know what I mean, Roger," Dr. Karpala said.

Thunder rolled. Roger shifted again.

It was raining that other day too; the day Lipton doesn't like to talk about. The day Dr. Karpala won't stop asking about...

This is where the dreamy, going back in time memory music would go.

They say extreme situations can make people fall in love. Well, that's what Lipton told obsidian-haired Annette once the dust settled in the catacombs. Lipton had always scoffed at the notion of archaeology being like a video game, but this expedition to find the lost catacombs of Z, whatever Z was, had been quite an adventure.

The dark, scary catacombs. The monsters. The iffy pizza delivery. Intense, indeed.

Through the chaos, though, there was her. Annette. The woman who made all this worthwhile. The two souls joined instantly; bodies as well, for Annette was quite a hugger. She tousled his hair affectionately. Lipton was smitten.

But then, abruptly, it was over.

Annette kept to herself, or more specifically, she kept to her sieve and brush. Her beautiful gray eyes were constantly downcast as she sifted through the sand for bits of physical history buried there. Gone were the longing looks, the mirthful eyes laughing at Lipton's crappy jokes.

"Annette, don't shut me out," Lipton pleaded.

Annette remained silent.

"Perhaps some men could coldly treat you as a specimen; a thing to be catalogued and studied."

Annette rolled her eyes at that.

Flustered, Lipton tried to rally and powered forward. "But Annette, my passion for you rivals even that of my work. I can't wall one off from the other. I must have you both. Can't you understand?"

Annette looked away, still silent.

"My heart is breaking, Annette. Would that I could live only by passion, remove this cursed brain from my head..."

This seemed to get Annette's attention. She looked at him, started to speak, but then tossed the sieve away and stood, back turned.

Lipton was frozen in place, torn by his own conflicting desires.

Annette slowly shuffled away. Out of necessity for his own sanity, Lipton's mind quickly erected a barrier between heart and brain.

***

But then, many weeks later, as Lipton catalogued some

specimens in his study, the front door of his flat burst open and his one true love - after archaeology - Annette, stood before him. The steel barrier between Lipton's heart and brain rusted away in joyful tears.

Their lovemaking was brutally intense and, honestly, quick. Still, Annette seemed nearly to fall to pieces in Lipton's arms. Lipton decided then and there that he could be a man of science AND a lover.

But soon, the walls started coming back.

Also, neighborhood pets started disappearing.

Annette would not even speak to Lipton. Dinners were silent affairs. She seemed to have no interest in food, always leaving her plates untouched.

"What's the matter, my love?" Lipton asked. But Annette just stared into space.

Lipton's trusted housekeeper, Estelle, stopped coming to work, but, oddly, left her car in the driveway until Lipton had it towed.

Annette, well, she was not the tidiest person, to be

honest. She left ragged bits of clothing everywhere. How was she so hard on her shirts? It frustrated the obsessively neat Lipton.

Their relationship wasn't all bad, though. Annette still laughed at his jokes, a hoarse dry laugh, but that was something. And Annette was an aggressive lover, passionately nibbling his face as they went at it.

But, over time, even this was not enough. Lipton wanted a life partner, not a bed partner. One day, he finally said, "Dearest, I'm going out." In the driveway, he mentally erected a wall between Annette and himself and drove straight to Dr. Karbala's office.

It was she who suggested Annette should join them for couple's therapy. Annette was not fond of riding in the car, clawed at the door and windows, but sat quietly during the session, eyeing Dr. Karbala intently.

Dr. Karbala removed her glasses and took Lipton's hand, smiling sadly. "Roger," she said, " I think it's time for you to face a simple truth."

"What do you mean, Doctor?" He searched the faces of Annette and Karbala for some clarity. One was blank. The other was a little sad.

"Roger," Karbala said, patting his hand, "your girlfriend is a zombie."

"The devil, you say!" Roger exclaimed. "Whatever do you mean?"

In one fluid motion, Annette leapt on Karbala's back, wrenched the head from Karbala's spinal column and sucked out the brains.

"Oh," Lipton said.

This story is from ATARI BYTES episode 159, inspired by the game Entombed. I may never – okay, will never – be asked to write an "Indiana Jones" adventure. This is what it might have looked like, so you know what you're missing.

DEATH BY THE NUMBERS:
A STEVE STETSON, 1980S SUPERSPY, ADVENTURE

San Francisco. The early morning hours. A nondescript warehouse.

Ivana Killyou circles a cot in the center of the room, illuminated only by a single bulb from an overhead light fixture. A tall man lies on the bed, moaning softy. His suit looks good though.

"You're running out of time, Mr. Stetson," Ivana Killyou says. "The poison works fast. Tell me: who do you work for?"

Stetson's head is swimming. It's like that time when he was eight and his dad made him smoke a cigarette. But he didn't want to smoke a cigarette, so his dad said, "Be a man," and lit up a Marlboro. It was gross and …

Focus, Stetson. Thoughts come to him slowly like running crap through a colander.

You'll be dead soon if you don't do something.

Stetson suddenly remembers where he is. San Francisco! They have earthquakes here, don't they? With all the strength he has, Stetson wills a small-scale earthquake to hit just this building right now.

And holy crap! It happens!

Stetson manages to roll off the cot and underneath it for cover as Ivana Killyou is knocked off her feet, then knocked out by debris.

The earthquake stops. All is silent. Stetson yanks Killyou's messenger bag from her slumped shoulders, finds the vial with the antidote and guzzles it down. He also swipes her coffee shop reward points card and a dog-eared copy of Raymond Carver's What We Talk About When We Talk About Love. "Still haven't read that one."

Rejuvenated, Stetson steps outside the warehouse, the only building hit by the freak earthquake. Stetson shrugs. "I told her I'd rock her world."

*This is where, in a movie, you would hear a

kickin' spy theme before the main plot of the movie starts.*

Stetson sat at the computer terminal. A light, but manly, sheen of sweat on his brow. "D....7," he said loudly into a microphone over the din of the klaxon warning of an imminent missile launch, then waited. When nothing happened, he murmured, "Damn."

"C 4," he grunted, realizing salmon wasn't a good color to wear on a day he might be pitting out.

Nothing.

"Stetson," Commander Maddie Grimm barked, "time is running out."

"Almost there, Maddie," Stetson said, eyes not leaving the screen, but reaching for a ham sandwich. Guy's gotta eat.

Through a mouthful of ham, he said into the microphone, "E 9."

That wasn't it either.

"This isn't looking good, Commander."

"Need I remind you, Stetson, the fate of the world is in your hands."

Stetson nodded. "Don't I know it." He frowned at a brown mustard stain on his Members Only jacket. "Awwww."

"Focus, Stetson," Grimm said, pacing now.

"F 2'" Stetson said, relief gently patting his face. "All right. Now we're getting somewhere."

"You have it?" Grimm's voice was hoarse with tension. Even the hairs on her fake fur hat were standing on end.

When the intonation of F3 got a desired effect, a jubilant Stetson asked if Grimm would like to have his baby. She ignored him, which is just generally good advice.

Maddie looked at the school gymnasium style, caged institutional clock on the concrete block wall and did not like what she saw. "Stetson, we need the override code. Now. Those missiles are about to launch."

Stetson cocked his head. "Code? Oh yeah, I finished that an hour ago." He snagged a scrap of paper off the corner of his desk. "Here you go."

Grimm's face remained, well, grim, but now it was overlaid with a shroud of disbelief monogrammed with disgust. "Then what the hell have you been doing?"

"Playing Battleship via dial up modem with Nick over in HR. These modem things are so cool. I wonder if you could send porn by computer."

Grimm was ready to unload, but Stetson waved a reassuring hand. "It's okay. I think I'm about to sink Nick's aircraft carrier."

Grimm peeled her hate-filled eyes away from Stetson and frowned at Stetson's chicken scratch on the paper. "What the hell is this nonsense?"

"Pig Latin," Stetson said. "It's okay. Only the most advanced code breakers know about it." He took the paper back from Grimm and recited:

"Ush-pay own-day irteen-thy imes-tay."

Maddie frowned. "What the hell is that?"

"Told you. Pig Latin," Stetson said. "Let me interpret. It means 'push down thirteen times'. It's a page out of the elevator repair manual."

"The elevator repair...? What are you talking about?"

"The best place to hide sensitive codes like missile launch and disarming codes is in a text no one reads," Stetson said, grinning. "No one, but yours truly."

"But how did you...?" Grimm's head was swimming.

"G-9," Stetson said into the microphone, then

to Grim, "Missile starts with M, which is the thirteenth letter of the alphabet, so I looked on page 13 and, obviously, Pig Latin is one of the hardest codes to crack - fitting for a missile code. But it's only hardest for anyone who isn't me. You press the down button for the elevator 13 times - M is thirteenth, remember - because you want to bring the missiles down. Obvious, really."

Grim just gaped at Stetson.

"You better hustle," Stetson said. "Wasting time." He leaned into the mic. "D-6."

Grim shook her head and sprinted to the elevator. "This is ridiculous," she repeated as she ran. But she hit the down button thirteen times in rapid succession. She crossed her fingers and various other body parts, desperately hoping to avoid Armageddon and also hoping no co-workers were watching.

The warning klaxon abruptly ceased. A computer monotone voice announced, "Missile Launch Aborted. All Clear." The lights came back up and all was quiet.

But all at once, Stetson let out a blood-curdling yell. Grimm sprinted back to the computer room. "What! What is it? More missiles!?"

Stetson beamed. "Nope. I just sank Nick's battleship."

"You're an idiot."

QUEUE THE SWEET STETSON MOVIE END THEME

This story from ATARI BYTES episode 160 is inspired by the game CODEBREAKER. Steve Stetson is a recurring, old-school spy character I use occasionally.

TO GO WHERE NO ONE HAS ...
BUT NOT BOLDLY

The gentle hum of the interstellar space vessel Cosmic's transporter beam powering up almost, but not quite, covered Commander Tomaliki's annoyed huffing.

"Move, team, move," Tomaliki said, gills flapping. "We can't wait any longer."

After a last check of their hand-held laser weapons, Lieutenants Quacklin and Orberst followed Tomaliki into the transporter device and particle beamed themselves onto the space station.

The hum of the Cosmic's transporter faded. The silence that followed was brief and soon replaced with a rapid-fire thud of heavy footfalls from the hallway. Ensign Kennedy Kendall burst into the empty room, heavy boots clanging on the deck.

She looked around desperately for her shipmates and saw no one. "Ooooohhh crap..." she said, foot-long eyelashes flittering nervously. "The captain is going to be soooo mad..."

Kendall considered going back to her quarters, maybe fake supernova flu. Or she could go to her duty station and say she was so engrossed in cataloging interstellar tape worms she forgot to meet the away team.

Kendall didn't know what to do. Her vestigial fish tail flapped indecisively.

The transporter control screen still flashed the coordinates the team had gone to. She could just pop on over and join the team. Maybe they wouldn't even notice. If they do question it, she could just tell them the zoology lab had some new ideas about categorizing the slime output of the cobalt bats infesting the space station as compared to common snotter-pillar populations found in the forests of Devon IV. By that point in the story, the away team would get bored and wander away – per the normal – and no one would question Kendall's tardiness.

Kendall reached out to activate the transporter. But she hesitated.

It's probably scary over there.

The snotter-pillar population on the space station was unlike any that humans had ever seen. They were super aggressive. Kendall didn't like aggressive creatures; not since that pushy four-headed Norigan at the academy had declared Kendall was to be her mate. She was only saved by the fact that only three of the Norigan's heads were into it. The Fourth head distracted the other three so Kendall could get away.

Anyway, the cobalt bats on the station had already killed a lot of the fleet. Same with the pods, the dirgins and the critters. Kendall studied creatures – like under a microscope or from behind some glass maybe.

She didn't go toe to vestigial appendage with them. She should really just go back to the lab; pretend Space Outlook put the appointment on the wrong day on her calendar or something.

Security Chief Loretta Bosch burst into the transporter room. "Kendall!" she said and tossed Kendall a laser weapon, which Kendall almost dropped. "The situation over there is becoming critical. The new modulation settings on that laser are done. You should get two, maybe three more shots with it. Get going."

"Aye, sir," Kendall said, barely audibly.

Bosch nodded and somehow burst out of the room.

Kendall looked at the transporter readout again. A trembling hand made its way to the "SEND" button.

And Kendall was on her way.

***

Kendall found herself in a cool, dimly lit secondary ventilation chamber; the station's back-up climate control area. The station was deadly quiet.

No, that's not quite true. In the distance, Kendall could hear weapons fire; mostly lasers, but some electric rifles and poofer guns too.

Kendall looked down at her weapon. Her hand was a little sweaty, so she switched the gun to her other hand, but that felt even weirder, so she switched back.

Kendall took a couple steps, then paused to check the power pack on the weapon, hoping perhaps she'd have to return to the ship to recharge. Nope, fully charged. Dammit.

Kendall heard Tomaliki shouting in the distance. Then a sonic grenade blast shook the station. Her crew mates needed help up there. Kendall set the weapon on maximum and...

...didn't go anywhere.

Instead, Kendall sat down right there on the floor among the dust bunnies that probably had more backbone than she did.

"I'm a space force officer," Kendall thought. "I'm not a coward."

So why couldn't she fight?

What good is a space force officer who is all about space – between the stars, in the lab, and the space between herself and others – but couldn't stomach the force part of the job?

Kendall wiped away a treacherous tear, felt a bit more sorry for herself than was the norm. In the distance, laser weapons fire mocked her.

Wait. What was that about stomaching stuff?

Kendall looked around, as if thoughts were bombarding her from outside like a gnat buzzing around.

Stomachs. Stomach lining. The creatures infesting the station had stomachs, sure. But they also had extremely high body temperatures. Kendall started frantically patting her uniform pockets, grateful to finally have space clothes that actually have pockets. She grinned, relieved, when she found what she was looking for. She held up the vial and squinted at its contents. Yep, there they were.

Kendall went to the climate control panel and turned

the heat way down. She waited a few, agonizing minutes then slowly, cautiously crept to the ventilation room's door. She first checked that the hallway was clear then emptied the contents of the vial into the hallway.

Kendall's idea was that by dropping the air temperature, the humans' body temperatures would drop. The temperatures of the creatures marauding through the space station would stay constant because of the unusual genetic make-up Kendall herself had helped define.

Space tape worms. That's what was in those vials she was carrying. Living space tape worms. By nature, tape worms attach to warm organisms. Kendall hoped they would ignore the humans and infest the invaders. The genetic incompatibility of the two would kill the invading creatures without firing a shot.

Well, without firing another shot.

The laser fire continued, though, for an agonizing amount of time. Kendall got a bit sleepy from boredom and cold. A dirgin rolled through the door before bumping Kendall's boot and coming to a stop. At first, Kendall sleepily pulled her foot away before some aspect of her space force training forced her to consciousness and then summoned all that training to... reach out and squash the dirgin under her boot. Then she cursed. "Aww," she said. "I wanted to see if the tapeworm would do it. Dammit."

Another fail...

But then the laser fight abruptly stopped. There was a quick exchange between the other space force officers. Most of it was indecipherable, except for Tomaliki declaring "All clear!"

"I guess it worked," Kendall whispered, and was pleased to find the sound didn't scare her. So she said it a bit louder. "I GUESS IT WORKED!" Had she just saved the space station?

"Crap. I got to get out of here." Kendall scrambled to her feet and smacked the transporter "SEND" button. Back on the Cosmic, she took her seat in the lab and prepared to resume her same old, anonymous life.

She'd always know what happened. That was enough for her.

This story inspired by ATARI BYTES episode 161: XENOPHOBE during a safari from the 2600 to the Atari 7800 system. That's right. On ATARI BYTES, we boldly go...well, you know where.

BAD POETRY CORNER:
ODE TO A GEAR SHIFT
OR FOUR LITTLE GEARS
OR 1,2,3,4 GEARS OF MY HEART

(Inspired by Schoolhouse Rock "A Noun is a Person, Place or Thing")

Well, the best auto racing you can know,
And the best racers that rev and go,
And any drivers their stuff do show,
You know they're dragsters.
A dragster always leads the herd,
A different kind of race you've heard,
I find it really just the thing,
To hear them shift gears one, two, three.

Oh, I've seen all kinds of races,
With runners wearing bright shoelaces.
Or gladiators in their chariots.
Saw lots of hares kick tortoise butts.

Oh, yeah, the joy does fill my face.

Well, every person you can know. (Like an accountant or a jazz singer.)

And every place that you can go. (Like a brewery. Or a podiatrist's office.)

And anything to which races you can show. (Like a mongoose. Or some sort of eel that lives at the bottom of the ocean and doesn't have eyes.)

You know they're race fans. Oh....

Mr. Soggy Pants is a clown uptown.

Has one of those little cars with all the other clowns.

We showed them how to read the tach.

Now they're squirting seltzer down the track.

Mr. Soggy pants is a clown...shifting down.

Well, every person you can know. (Leprechauns, or Trekkies, or bee keepers)

And every place that you can go. (Like the moon. Or the Sears tower.)

And anything to which races you can show. (Like mollusks. Or the talking car from Knight Rider)

You know they're race fans. Oh...

The drivers downshifted their dragsters, set 'em free.

My best friend was waitin' roadside for me. (He brought the popcorn.)

We waited at the finish line you know,

For the roaring engines there to go.

When the drivers downshifted their dragsters, set 'em free.

Well every person you can know. (Like champion hog callers or bus boys)

And every place that you can go. (Like Pebble Beach. Or the canned cat food aisle)

And anything to which races you can show. (Like your third cousin. Or Ringo Starr.)

You know they're race fans.

VROOM.

From "Bad Poetry Corner" in ATARI BYTES episode 162, inspired by the game DRAGSTER.

KANGA-RUINED

At only four months old, Joseph "Joey" Kangaroo already had a mean left hook. His little paw packed a punch Mama Kangaroo knew would serve him well in the weird life of the Roos. There might never be anyone faster than Joey…except Mama herself.

Mama and Joey shadow-boxed in a clump of eucalyptus trees. "That's it, boy," Mama said. "Don't drop your right."

The boy grinned and swung a playful right at his mother, who dodged the sneak attack easily. "And don't telegraph your moves, son. That'll get you killed."

"Killed by who, Mama?" Joey asked, for he had never quite understood that.

Mama Kangaroo licked at a scratch on her flank as she considered how to answer. "Could be anyone. You just never know. Gotta always be ready."

"Daddy always said we should trust each other."

Mama Kangaroo nodded, old sorrows creeping up before being kicked back down. "Yes, he did. And now he's gone. So guess that didn't do much good."

The screechy whoops of the monkeys in the trees chilled Mama Kangaroo's tired bones. Joey didn't know why. The sound didn't scare him, but Mama's reaction did.

"Was that...?" Joey started to ask, but the question was drowned out by the warning call of a didgeridoo echoing through the outback.

Mama was immediately on high alert. The familiar blanket of Australian heat was whisked off every living thing, replaced just as quickly with a freezing blanket of darkness.

"Into your pouch," Mama said. Joey didn't like it. Mama's voice was low and forceful. A stern look from Mama sent Joey diving for cover inside Mama's pouch. Joey climbed into the recesses of the pouch; down the narrowest corridor, past the arcade, across from the sundae bar. She wasn't punishing him; Joey knew that. She was...afraid?

Mama bounded away. The monkey sounds were coming closer.

Where were they going? Soon, he had the sensation Mama was…climbing? Kangaroos don't climb. What game was this? Joey opened all the dead bolts and poked his head from the pouch for a look.

A fusillade of apples rained down on them as Mama climbed up and across a series of platforms. What kind of tree was this?

"Keep your head down," Mama directed.

But then Mama stumbled, slamming hard on metal scaffolding. Joey tumbled from the pouch into blinding light and foreign structures. He'd never seen trees like this…

"Run," Mama shouted and, like a reflex, Joey did. Fast as his mother, he bounded across the platform, no idea where he was going.

Joey gasped and twisted away as monkey paws clawed at him from the underside of the scaffold.

Apples like gunshots exploded around him.

The monkeys chattered incessantly. Mocking. Calling.

It was hard to tell. A monkey leapt from somewhere above and landed on Joey. He screamed and suddenly Mama was there with an upper cut that sent the monkey flying. But then two more landed on Mama.

Mama and Joey together beat the monkeys back. But then Mama shoved Joey back into the pouch with such force, he nearly knocked the Ming vase off the coffee table.

That's when a gorilla leapt from the highest platform and plowed into Mama. "Joey is ours," the gorilla said.

"Why?" Mama said. "What the hell are you and the monkeys even doing here?" The gorilla responded with a brutal punch, which Mama returned in kind.

One last roundhouse kick, followed by a misstep, sent gorilla and kangaroo plunging from atop the scaffold. The sudden landing knocked all the artwork off the walls of Joey's pouch.

A bell clanged in the distance. Joey didn't know what a bell was, but knew that it signaled...something.

He didn't hear the monkey chatter anymore. Joey wondered if he should venture out. He hazarded a peek…

There were lights outside. Did the monkeys come back? He could hear them chattering.

No, wait, this chatter was different. Not monkeys. Not Roos. What where they? Joey hid in a cedar closet.

The animal rescue service approached Mama Roo. "That's a shame," a bearded man muttered and called over his partner.

Joey didn't, couldn't, understand what was happening. He sensed his mother was dead. What that meant for his future was unclear.

He would be fed and cared for. He would be all right. But he would never be the same.

Inspired by ATARI BYTES episode 163: KANGAROO. Okay. This is a weird one. I doubt even knowing this game would help.

LOST AND FOUND

"Because you're a dolt, that's why."

Gary laughed and set his backpack down, jostling the water bottle, which rolled down a couple steps cut into the limestone walkway. "I'm a 'dolt'? Where the hell did you pull that from?" He laughed again.

Brent shifted his weight and considered how to respond. It infuriated him when Gary brought out that laugh; the mocking one. Brent also hated that it was making him pout like the child Gary was implying he was. It was all Brent could do to not shout, "Don't tell me what to do. I am not a child."

No matter how close you are to your partner, 24/7 for a whole week is a long time to spend with someone. This week of driving through endless miles of Midwestern farmland interspersed with tourist destinations, frenetic sight-seeing and eating every damn meal together was taking its toll.

Moving on as if the argument was inconsequential, Gary said, "We're falling behind the group. We should catch up."

"Fine,", Brent said with a tone. "Just -" He paused, patted all the pockets of his khaki shorts. "Shit. I left my phone somewhere."

"Seriously?" Gary said, a bit more sternly than intended, or maybe not.

"Not like I did it on purpose, you know," I'm pretty sure it's on the ledge near that pretty little waterfall. What if it falls in, Gary?"

"Well, go get it," Gary said. "Clock's tickin',"

"Yeah, yeah." Brent stood and groaned, rubbing his knee. "My knee is killing me. These stone floors...Gary, could you...?"

Gary groaned.

"Please? I've already slowed us down enough."

"Whatever," Gary grunted and turned back toward the trail they'd just come up on, heavy footfalls echoing behind him, each step like an auditory obscene gesture to Brent.

Gary took the time back to the waterfall to reexamine some of the contours of this cavern, shaped by thousands of years of rainwater runoff. The park service had recently switched to LED lighting to avoid algae growth on light bulbs. "Why would anything want to live down here?" Gary muttered.

The lights were more strategically placed to highlight different contours of the caverns. Gary approached a split in the trail. One way was the marked tourist trail. The other way had a sign warning people to stay out.

But Gary was so enamored with looking at the lights that it took a moment for his eyes to register when the lights went out, eliciting a startled whoop from a sixty-year-old bank teller in the tour group up ahead.

Mildly disoriented, Gary kept walking…but down the wrong path.

Within moments, the lights came back up, briefly blinding Gary again. He blinked at rock formations that pretty much looked like all the other rock formations. He had the uneasy feeling he was going the wrong way, but he found the going itself - away from Brent for a few moments - easy enough that he kind of didn't mind.

In the shadowy periphery, he thought he might have seen a mass... a blob?...hugging the wall tight. But that was ridiculous. And by the time he turned his head for another look, it was gone anyway.

Farther down the path, the trail split again. Gary didn't remember a second split when he came through with Brent initially, but he kept going, confident in his sense of direction.

He could still walk upright, but Gary's hair just brushed the top of this tunnel, which spanned thirty feet or so. The only light came from the LED's on either end. The slight movement of hair against limestone, compelled him to brush his hair lightly with his fingers.

As he walked, something tickled Gary's neck. He reached back to adjust his polo shirt collar and felt what he thought was his shirt tag.

But it moved.

So, not a tag then.

Gary snatched his hand back. A dime-sized spider

crawled on his palm and Gary flung it away with a yelp. He was glad no was here to hear.

Now his left arm tingled. Another spider, quarter-sized this time, did laps around his elbow. He flapped that arm like a chicken wing, not caring when he smacked the cavern wall.

Gary held his phone up to the ceiling of this tunnel, the screen illumination was just enough to reveal it was covered in spiders.

Gary sprinted for the other end of the tunnel. Once there, the scream that erupted from his lungs put the earlier yelp to shame. He barely even register the warm, moist thud as his knee crunched into the midsection of a three-foot spider waiting there, prompting it to fold into a ball and roll into a dark corner, lethal venom meant for Gary instead just leaving a shiny trail behind it as Gary kept running. Gary wiggled as he ran, attempting to dislodge any more passengers.

Finding himself now in a wide chamber, a sound caught Gary's attention. When you're anticipating hearing something specific, say a rushing waterfall splashing a lost cellphone, it can take a moment for the brain to process that the sound you actually hear is not that sound. In this case, it took two moments for Gary to process that what he actually heard was the whirr-click of robotic machinery. Unfortunately, that was one moment too many.

Gary was now surrounded by robots.

Some of the robots had the standard one head. Others had two. Scores of beady red eyes focused on him. All were firing laser blasts as Gary bobbed and weaved. "Brent can look for his own damn phone," Gary screamed.

The lasers actually made the pew-pew noise like in the movies. He couldn't help noticing the two headed bots' shots hit closer than the one-head bots'. "Whadaya know?" Gary heard himself shout. "Two heads really are better than one." A volley of appreciative laser blasts came in response.

Another tunnel. Gary tripped over a box of bullets. Just bullets. No gun. "What am I supposed to do with these?" Gary shoved a handful of ammo into his pocket anyway.

No spiders in this tunnel, thankfully. But where could he go?

"Wish you were here, Brent," Gary thought. He hated that it was looking pretty likely the last time he saw

Brent was in a fight.

With lurching, heavy steps, a robot appeared at the tunnel entrance. Time to go.

Gary sprinted through the other end of the tunnel.

The blob swirled itself around Gary's feet as the robots circled around. This was the end. Gary was sure of it.

Once, on a trip to the beach, Gary started choking on a bit of snow cone. It's an odd thought, choking on a bit of frozen water; presumably it would melt and all would be good. But not this time. Maybe there was a congealed lump of cherry syrup or something. Gary always wondered about that, the choking. How could that happen?

Anyway, when he was choking, Gary was alone that time too. Brent had gone off to find another shovel - Brent was a really good sandcastle builder - and Gary lay there gasping. He was trying, and failing, to wrench enough air from his lungs to call out Brent's name. A ten-year-old wearing water wings had to apply the Heimlich.

This day, surrounded by robots from god-knows-where, Gary made up for that other horrible day, applying the full power of his respiratory and vocal systems to scream out Brent's name.

The robots, of course, didn't give a crap. Gary tried to prepare himself to die.

Gary's mental preparations, which mostly involved saying over and over, "Yep. This is it." were disrupted as a particularly large spider from the tunnel crawled from his collar, down the front of his shirt and sat on one of the three buttons there. A good three of the spider's legs seemed to wave "hello".

Gary gasped, but then he had an idea.

The winter before last, the diagnostic sensors on the Tesla went wonky. Brent seemed fine with not knowing if he had a low tire unless the dashboard told him so. But Gary insisted on getting the problem diagnosed. It turned out, mice had crawled into the engine for warmth, mucking up the electrical system.

In this moment before his death, Gary had a seemingly much different problem to solve, but, he realized, it might not be that different at all.

Grimacing, Gary grabbed the spider from his chest - the little spiky hairs on its back were surprisingly soft. He set the spider on the nearest robot's foot, where it immediately crawled into the narrow space around the ankle joint.

In seconds, the robot started spasming, twisting, break dancing and doing the funky chicken. Then he collapsed in a pile of rivets.

Gary made full advantage of the opening in the kill-Gary circle and made for a tunnel that looked like maybe it was an exit, hands over his head as if that would protect him from the fusillade of laser blasts erupting around him.

As he ran into yet another tunnel, Gary shoved the handful of bullets from the ammo box into a small crevice in the wall, then bolted into the tunnel out of this chamber.

A robot laser blast struck the bullets, exploding the gunpowder. The blast caused an avalanche of limestone, sealing the robots into the chamber.

Gary ran. Ran some more. He was not slowed down at all by the hitch in his knee from that rock wall climbing accident when he stopped mid ascent to take a selfie. "Told you I'm fine, Brent," he muttered. "Orthopedist, my ass."

Finally, Gary found a familiar tunnel.

And there was Brent. Gary had never been so happy to see anyone. Beaming, he ran up to Brent, who said only...

"Did you find my phone?"

"What?" Gary said. "Oh. Uh, no, But listen..."

"I need that phone, Gary. It's brand new."

"Yeah, but Brent, you won't believe."

Brent sighed and made that face that says, "I'm pretending to listen, but I'm not trying very hard."

Gary poured out the whole story of his adventure in the excruciating detail he was fond of.

Brent just nodded. "That must have been...weird," he

said.

"You don't believe me," Gary said.

"Of course, I do."

"No," Gary declared, arms crossed. "You don't."

"Well...it is a little hard to believe," Brent admitted." But I love and trust you. If you say it happened, then it did."

Gary studied each word out of Brent's mouth, rolled each syllable, weighing and evaluating the veracity of Brent's assertion. Did he really believe or was he just humoring Gary? Really, though, he was too happy to be alive to care.

"Sorry about your phone, though," Gary said.

"It's just a phone."

They both shrugged. "Well, we should get going I guess," Gary finally said.

"I'll just re pack my things." Only now, Gary noticed the contents of Brent's back pack were strewn across the cave floor.

"Right," Brent said.

Gary trotted ahead to catch up with the rest of the tour group. Brent lingered, repacking. "Gary, you're so sweet. So good-hearted."

Brent removed the robot remote control device from his pocket, sent the self-destruct order and disabled the device, chucking it into a nearby waterfall. Brent really did like waterfalls.

Brent sneered in direction of his companion. "But you really ARE a dolt."

Inspired by ATARI BYTES EPISODE 165: DARK CAVERN. And waterfalls.

IT'S PEOPLE I CAN'T STAND
...BUT I CAN STAND WITH THEM

The bunker door slammed open with the heavy *ker-chung* of steel on steel. Two unshaven space force enlisted men, both young, barely out of Space Force School, cautiously peered out. The gorgeous, star-filled night was belied by the blasts of the invading alien fleet in the distance. Here and now, though, it seemed relatively safe.

The men stepped out of the bunker, hoisting a gurney between them. "You sure about this?" the much taller, slightly younger one said.

"Doc says it's the only thing for 'im. The war effort comes first, eh?" the shorter one replied. "Let's get on with it."

"Poor bastard," the first one said, lowering his end of the gurney.

The other cadet did the same and they set about undoing the straps that bound Archie McManigle. He started to stir as the sedative wore off and the cadets scurried back inside, sliding the massive bunker door shut behind them.

Waking now, Archie McManigle, age 43, beamed at the open sky above, even as alien ships moved ever closer.

FIVE HOURS EARLIER...

The gentle beeps and blips of monitors wired to the man in the bed seemed to part like an ocean flowing around Olivia as she swept into the room. "I got here soon as I could," Olivia said. "Traffic was intense. I took the #9 to the #14. The tunnel at Ridgeway was clogged with soldiers waiting for transport to the battle zones. Everywhere is so crowded these days."

I curse this damn war," Jack said. 'But the energy in the air is electrifying."

"And not just because of laser battles," Olivia said, setting down her latte ration and government issued air horn.

A quiet, little laugh.

Then Olivia looked down at the clean-shaven face of her dear, if eccentric friend lying in the bed and asked, "How is he?"

The monitor noises burbled to the surface once more. Jack took a deep breath. Some of the hairs in his luxuriant beard were caught in the updraft.

"Who knows?" Jack said. "The doctors sure don't. Archie was down in the marketplace when someone stepped on his foot. No big deal, happens all the time in the bunker. That's why we have government issue steel toed boots. But Archie had a meltdown. He was gasping for air, sweating, swatting at people. People moved in to try and calm him down. He had some sort of seizure. People backed off and the seizure stopped."

Olivia shook her head. The light flickered as the invading forces shook the bunker with their laser cannons. "Why put straps on him?" She asked.

"Well, when the med techs brought Archie into the infirmary, he woke up, leapt from the gurney and hugged General Fitzhugh, while screaming, "I know how to end this war." Unfortunately, at the time, the general was in the middle of his twice weekly sperm exam and did not appreciate the interruption."

"The leader of the resistance is taking time out for fertility treatment?"

"No," Jack said. "He just likes to take the little guys out for a run now and then. Anyway, the general had Archie sedated, strapped down and brought here."

Dr. Genevieve Queenly entered the room wearing the expression of a woman who has seen it all and is bored by most of it. She was trailed by duckling-like interns and the small room filled up fast.

The monitors taped to Archie beeped faster and the interns scribbled intently on their electronic devices.

On a gesture from Dr. Queenly, she and the interns stepped back two paces. Archie's vitals leveled at almost normal. Dr. Queenly nodded in silent confirmation of her own, earlier diagnosis. She did that a lot.

"What's going on with him, Doctor?" Olivia asked.

Dr. Queenly looked dramatically into the middle distance. It was a long bit of drama. Olivia got impatient. Jack got uncomfortable. He hated awkward silences. He was known to have wet his pants on more than one elevator ride.

Finally, Dr. Queenly said, "I'm afraid your friend Archie has suffered a massive..." - more dramatic pausing - "...space attack."

Jack gasped. And a particularly well-timed explosion overhead punctuated the moment. No one took much notice, though. Life in the bunker was often punctuated with explosions.

Olivia cocked her head. "You're making that up. If you don't know what's wrong with him, say so."

Though seemingly impossible, Dr. Queenly's frown sank even lower. She did not enjoy explaining things. "It's a phenomenon that has developed since society moved into the bunker to escape the devastation outside. For some, the close quarters we live in invigorates them. They feed off it; are stimulated by being surrounded by so many. For others, these crowded conditions have an opposite effect. They go... mad. Complete rejection of society sometimes."

"Archie isn't rejecting society," Olivia objected. "He's just nerdy."

At that, Archie sat bolt upright. The monitors seemed to scream at the disruption. He didn't actually make it all the way up; about forty five degrees maybe before the arm straps pulled him back down.

Shouting to be heard, Archie sang, "All by myself/ Don't wanna be/ All by myself /anymore..." He paused and said, "That's a crock. I'd love to be all by myself. Think of all the waffles." Archie laughed for a full thirty seconds. It made Jack really uncomfortable.

The laughter choked in Archie's throat as the interns - pens and pads in hand - moved in closer, trying to see if Archie actually had a stitch in his side.

Archie shook and gasped until Dr. Queenly injected him with something she would only call, "Just something I whipped up over the lunch hour. I call it 'Syringe Surprise.'"

The surprise, it turned out, was just that it was a tranquilizer that knocked Archie out.

Dr. Queenly turned to the nearest intern - "We'll implement quarantine protocol".

Now the intern gasped. It was a pretty good gasp, Jack thought.

"Wait," Archie said, coming to. "Quarantine sounds like more confined spaces." A quick grunt and Archie snapped one, then the other strap that held him to the bed. He bolted from the room.

Archie ran the halls of the bunker, eluding capture for hours. He desperately wanted somewhere that the walls wouldn't close in on him, where he wouldn't feel so alone surrounded by so many. The thing about a bunker, though, is that while it keeps the violence out, it locks the fear in.

And it was at that point, that Archie McManigle had a brilliant idea. Also a splitting headache because the chief of security clubbed him over the head for trespassing in the bunker's bocce ball arena.

The quarantine protocol was initiated. Olivia was detained for interference with official acts and Jack was fined for public urination. Both would do a week or two; sentenced to deodorizing the bunker. But for now, they had bigger problems.

Alone outside the bunker now, Archie looked up at the sky, stars intermittently pock-marked with squadron after squadron of would-be enemy invaders. Every so often, a laser array from the planetary defense would release a laser bolt.

"I hate people," Archie muttered, then corrected himself. "I love mankind," he clarified. "It's people I can't stand." He wondered where he'd heard that before. No matter. He hoped the invaders felt the same.

Archie, who'd always been good at climbing, scaled the laser array; the way lighted by the enemy flares around him. Oddly, they didn't shoot at him.

When Archie tap-tap-tapped on the control booth window at the top of the array, the startled gunner there didn't quite know what to do. His mother, though, had always told him not to be rude. So, he rolled down the window.

Archie climbed in, shoved his way to the communication console and radioed the general in command. When he explained what he wanted the general to do, the general was…dubious. But, frankly, the planet was going down. The planet's own squadrons had taken heavy losses. The controls that came with the new ships were awkward and hard to use. The shipment of adapters to make the old controllers work with the new ships had been delayed.

So, the general said, "Sure. Why the hell not?"

An hour later, the entire population of the bunker, all ten thousand of them, poured out through the gate and stood in the wasteland that had once been a national park, locked hands and stared up at the enemy ships above.

Archie and Jack were uneasy, on many levels. Olivia rolled her eyes, certain they were going to die in the stupidest way. Dr. Queenly did not approve of this.

The general gave the order to his soldiers to put down their weapons and they reluctantly did so.

All the people just stood. Waiting. Inviting devastation or vindication for their - sometimes reluctant – belief that if the enemy could see who they were shooting at, they might not do so.

The invaders' lasers fell silent. The whole planet, in fact, fell silent. The silence was overwhelming.

Jack dribbled a little from his nethers.

Archie tried to hum a little through clenched teeth. He was happy, though, when no one joined him because that would make this corny moment even cornier.

The general assumed any moment now that the invaders would open fire any moment and wipe them all out. At least if they were all destroyed, there would be no one to remember him as the bonehead general that screwed the planet.

But then, as you've no doubt predicted, the enemy ships, one by one, engaged hyperspace engines and left this quadrant of space. Would they be back? Probably. This, at least, gave some breathing room to open one-on-one negotiations of peace. And the general knew just who would be drafted to lead those negotiations. He looked over at Archie McManigal who, at that moment, was doing the funky chicken and periodically joyfully licking Jack's and Olivia's cheeks.

Well, maybe the provisional government could get another negotiator. Dr. Queenly maybe…or maybe not.

At least they were still alive. For now. String together enough nows and you've got a future.

Inspired by episode 166: SPACE ATTACK. Still hoping I can get an adult diaper company to sponsor the podcast.

UNTITLED DIPLOPODA-BASED COMEDY PILOT PITCH MEETING

Hollywood agent Bernie Bernest sighed from deep within his soul when his secretary Alice told him which client was on hold. Bernie thought himself to be a pretty good agent - only a couple of his clients had been fired off movies for doing coke on set.

But this client...oi. Well, better get it over with. Bernie picked up the receiver and hit the button. "Winston!" Bernie said cheerfully as he could. "How's my favorite client?"

Bernie winced as he caught an earful from his "favorite" client.

"Winston...Winston...listen to me. The producers are dying to meet you. You're perfect for this part. The whole show would be built around you. So it's a sitcom, so what? Look at The Cosby Show. People love that guy."

Bernie drummed his fingers on his desk as Winston unleashed another fusillade. When there was a break, Bernie said, "Let me blunt, Winston. You know I love you. And I love artsy films as much as the next guy. But the tony producers ain't callin', Winston. These guys are. It's 1984 and you haven't worked since 1982. You need this."

The call concluded and Bernie the agent leaned back in his chair. Even the dulcet tones of George Michael couldn't lower his blood pressure. Cufflinks glinted under the office lighting as he rubbed his eyes. His secretary's shoulder pads barely fit through the doorway as she brought him two aspirin and a Perrier. Was the prestige of Hollywood worth all this?

***

The juice bar at the *Pump It Up Gym and Fitness Center* was a popular spot to hang out after jazzercize class. The room was a rainbow of neon leotards and headbands. So much blow-dried hair flowed around the room, it was like a rolling sea of hair sprayed fuzz.

At the center table sat a guy in sunglasses and an argyle sweater and another guy in sunglasses with a cape. Not like a Superman cape; like a cape that supposedly was once, but in reality probably never was, in fashion.

Bernie and Winston met outside and studied their prey through the windows. "Okay," Bernie said. "Let me do the talking. That's my job, right? This sitcom gig is ours."

"Bill, Ted," Bernie said to the men when he and his client strode purposefully into the juice bar. Bernie shook hands and took a seat opposite Bill. Winston slowly eased into the seat opposite Ted.

"What have you got for us, Ted?" Bernie asked as he tucked into the bean sprouts and tofu medley on the table, immediately regretting it.

"I think my most excellent partner, Bill can explain better," Ted said.

"Thank you, Ted." He turned to Bernie and Winston. "Okay, dudes, this new show is most righteous."

Bernie didn't remember Bill and Ted being quite so... like this. Maybe he was having a stroke. It wouldn't be the first time.

Ted was still talking.

"Right, so this show is like *'Green Acres'* meets *'A-Team'* meets *'Knight Rider'*."

Bill shook his head. "Maybe not *'Knight Rider'*."

"Right," Ted said. "Definitely not *'Knight Rider'.*"

A woman with tight curls down to her shoulders and a lime green leotard refilled the carrot juice glasses on the table - none of which were touched - as "Let's Get Physical" queued up on the juice bar's boom box.

"You, Winston," Ted continued, "will play the leader of a rag-tag army of millipedes in an uneasy alliance with the humans to defend the garden from the spiders, beetles, dragonflies and all sorts of other creatures who want to devour the veggies within."

Bernie cocked his head. "Real veggies or props?" He asked.

"Some practical props. Some model work. Whatever looks best on videotape."

"Soundstage or on location?"

"Little of both," Bill said. "Whatever the episode calls for. Within budget, of course. And the budget is most excellent "

Ted elbowed Bill in the ribs.

"But budgets are budgets," Bill said.

Winston whispered to his agent, who nodded.

"What sort of billing does Winston get?" Bernie asked.

"Well," Ted said. "He's totally the star, dude."

Bill clarified. "We're totally stroking Hasselhoff for the human lead, but your big screen fame will no doubt get you righteous top billing."

Winston whispered to his agent again.

Bernie smiled at Bill and Ted. "Right. Well, let's get to the point. We have some concerns about Winston playing essentially a comedic part. He's a dramatic actor. In films."

Ted cocked his head. "But he hasn't done a film in h\ years, has he?" The tone was light…but perhaps not light enough.

Winston slowly inched forward, upending one of the carrot juices, staring at Ted.

Bill raised a calming hand. "Now. Now. We're all fans here. Winston, you know we loved you in Wrath of Khan. Your portrayal of that slug still gives me chills."

"I. Was. A. Ceti. Eel," Winston hissed. "Tell him, Bernie." Winston left a trail of indignant slime as he slid away; his exit back across the table was marred by an unfortunate stumble into the little tray where they put the coffee sweeteners.

Winston crawled back to his stool and sulked on an orange peel.

"Dudes," Ted said. "We want to be in the Winston business. This could be a great move for him. You know that. It's a dirty little secret that slugs in Hollywood don't get the respect they deserve."

"Word," Bill said, nodding.

Bernie cringed. "He really doesn't like to be called a slug."

"Not a slug," Winston called from across the room, emitting a lot of volume from such a small set of lungs.

"This is his time to shine," Ted said. "He's a righteous dude. The world needs to see that, my friend."

Bernie nodded. "Well, what if we talk money..."

Bill and Ted shared a collective, pained look. "Yeah, well, here's where things get a little heinous," Bill said. "You know how Hollywood is. All this money around, but still budgets are tight. Everything is so expensive. This millipede show will be filled with excellent special effects and elaborate battles that will look most excellent on screen. But that costs money. And that means less money for the actors, unfortunately."

"Bogus," Ted muttered.

"So," Bill said, smiling broadly. "The money isn't great. But I think we can make top billing happen on a major network, prime time event series and your client can stretch from righteous drama to action comedy."

"Everybody loves the action comedies," Ted said. "He'll be a star again."

At the word 'again', both Bill and Bernie cringed.

Displaying a new skill he should put on his acting resume along with horseback riding and fencing, Winston the ceti eel soared across the room and inserted himself in Ted's right ear canal.

Ted gasped, sweated, tried to keep the words in, but finally blurted, "We're desperate. There are no other millipede type beings in Hollywood. If Winston doesn't say yes to this project, the millipede show is dead and Bill and I are back to selling vacuums door to door."

"Whooooaaaa," Bill said

Now Bernie grinned. He took a long draw of carrot juice as if it was brandy. It wasn't. He leaned forward. "Gentlemen, let's talk money…"

Inspired by "Millipede" from episode 167 of ATARI BYTES. Also, the 1980s. And possibly a fever dream.

I'VE GOT A LOVELY BUNCH OF COCONUTS... BUT IS THAT ALL THERE IS TO LIFE?

The jungle shook as the mighty Cal Best stamped his massive feet, beating his chest and roaring to the heavens. HE was the true king of the jungle.

The jungle hunter approached. Cal Best knew he was supposed to be afraid, but the little man was so small, so inconsequential, he could not muster even a bit of fake fear.

The jungle hunter clung to a massive lily pad in a swamp. "See here," the hunter said, "I'll tolerate no more of this foolishness." His walrus mustache belied his poor swimming ability as the jungle hunter slipped from the lily pad into a pile of rhino muck. This made Cal Best laugh even harder.

Seeing that Cal Best was laughing, his hippo and rhinoceros minions felt safe to laugh too.

Still chucking coconuts, Cal Best roared, "Take them! Take them all! Soon, as with the mighty armies of old, this land will quake from coconuts rumbling forth. And I…1 shall deliver coconuts to the four corners and, in that way, claim dominion over all."

The jungle hunter pleaded, "Please, Cal Best, your coconut distribution path is unparalleled. No other jungle king can keep up."

Cal Best became furious. "Other jungle king? There is no other jungle king? There is only CAL BEST. I deliver more coconuts to more minions who benefit from my largesse.

The jungle alert system sounded; a weird mix of "The Lion King" and that noise fingernails make on a chalkboard.

Startled, Cal Best looked frantically over his shoulder. Where was this strange noise coming from? He looked up at Massive Mountain. Yes, it was speaking to him, but what was it trying to say? The voice of the mountain only rang through the land in times of great strife. In times when all of creation was in peril. Cal Best knew this message must be significant.

"Cal," the voice intoned. "It is time…"

Cal's mind swam, floated through the ether, back in time.

Cal Bestosian banged his head against the overhead compartment of his cubicle as he regained consciousness. It is time? Time for what? Dream world and real world slugged it out for control. And, as always, reality won.

He sometimes regretted setting his laptop to chime every time an email came in. On one hand, it pierced the corporate gloom of this cubicled wing of Love Your Coconuts, Inc. This company had not embraced open-concept office seating arrangements. On the other hand, the cheerful little chirp of an arriving email usually belied the digital crap-flow from the regional coconut distributor that had just arrived in Cal's in box. As assistant to the regional coconut distributor, Cal had very little power, a moderate amount of responsibility, except for the interesting stuff like corporate retreats and what not, and a whole lot of crap that flowed like coconut milk down the mountainside.

Mountainside? What made Cal think of that analogy? Anyway...

The email was a reminder that the video conference was about to start. Cal clicked on the conferencing app; a small gesture that nevertheless signaled a monumental surrender to banal reality.

The regional coconut distributor's big, dumb mustache filled the screen. The world asserted itself.

But did Cal insert an animated coconut into the conference screen over the regional distributor's head that every once in a while he could pop like a zit, sending a satisfying spray of animated coconut milk all over that stupid conference. Yes. Yes, he did.

Yes, the real world always wins. But the dream world never dies.

Inspired by ATARI BYTES episode 168: CONGO BONGO, and totally not by the futility of office life.

ONCE MORE 'ROUND THE TRACK

ONCE UPON A TIME…

Grady Grand Prix started his life as a mini race track spanning the distance between the refrigerator and the cupboard with all those pots and pans that were so fun to bang.

Toddler Samantha spent hours with the little fat fingers of one hand gripped tightly around the thick, rubber roof of a red toy dump truck and the other hand clutching a green station wagon type thing with a smiling grille and eyes for headlights. Samantha pushed the two toys back and forth, back and forth, occasionally smashing them together, with very little progress being made around the track. But she was having fun and Grady was pleased.

Eventually, Samantha grew. And, like her, Grady Grand Prix grew too. Samantha and her friends rode their banana-seat bicycles from one end of the street to the other. None of them was old enough to go around the block unescorted yet, but that didn't stop them from wearing safety-pinned beach towels that flowed in the breeze like the capes of the superheroes the kids thought they were.

When Samantha was a teenager, Grady was a little-used flat stretch of concrete behind the cement plant. Samantha would put the Chevette in gear and take off. Sometimes Eric would race her in his mom's Ford, but Samantha was happy to make the runs alone. But a near miss with a minivan and a ticket for reckless driving as she flew back into town was enough to put her back on a bicycle for a while.

Grady was sad. There were lots of cars on the road and all of them had drivers Grady could watch out for, but none of those cars were Samantha's Chevette and none of those drivers were Samantha. Grady cared for all of them – did his best to make sure there were no bumps that could hurt the cars or trash that could cause the cars to swerve. But it just wasn't the same.

Eventually, Samantha's mom let Samantha have her keys back. Grady did a dance for joy, buckling the concrete and toppling a truck full of cream-filled snack cakes, but no one was hurt.

Samantha, though, became a super-cautious driver. It took forever for her to get places. Grady felt less like a racetrack and more like a parking lot. No offense to parking lots. Some of Grady's best friends were parking lots.

All that was about to change though.

One night during her second semester of college, some of Samantha's friends convinced her to go with them to the local speedway to watch the stock cars. The sounds of the engines, the smell of burnt rubber, the roaring crowd; all of it was intoxicating. Wait. That might have been the three tallboys she consumed.

Anyway, riding home that night, all Samantha could think about was getting behind the wheel on the track. Grady hummed a happy tune, that was quickly drowned out by Guns 'n Roses on the car's radio.

Samantha loved stock car racing. Grady racetrack liked it fine too. But there was something…missing. Samantha won a few trophies and was waiting to move on. But to do what? She considered becoming a professional NASCAR racer, but then one day at a family reunion, she walked by her grandpa who was parked in front of the TV playing the Sears Tele-Games console.

"What'cha doin', Grandpa?' Samantha asked.

"What?" Grandpa shouted, jabbing grumpily at the overlay on the controller. He didn't hear well, but mostly he just had an attitude.

"What game is it?" Samantha said, louder this time.

"Auto racing," Grandpa barked. "These formula one cars are the only true form of racing." His little red car skidded into one of the beige walls on the screen. "Dagnabbit," Grandpa said, chucking his empty PBR can across the room.

Samantha walked away, the wheels spinning – both behind her on the screen and in her brain. Formula One? That would be something different.

A few calls and a few called-in favors with her racing buddies later, Samantha found herself strapped into the one-person cockpit of her own formula one racer. Low to the ground and built for speed, the car was the automotive equivalent of Samantha herself.

Samantha whooped with joy as she roared around Grady Grand Prix racetrack.

Grady loved the feel of hot rubber against his asphalt again, but he was a little nervous that this racetrack seemed to be no-holds-barred. Filthy oil slicks stained Grady's straightaways. Cars kept sailing off the bridges. Why are there bridges on a racetrack? Was all this in the grand prix instruction manual? Did a grand prix instruction manual even exist? Some days, Grady wished he was a simple country road where not much ever happened.

But Samantha was happy. So Grady was happy too.

Eventually in a truncated amount of time for story purposes, Samantha conquered grand prix racing. She retired from driving and became a formula one team owner instead.

In time, the formula one racetrack closed. Grady enjoyed the quiet for a while. But every time the rusty hinge on the locked gate at the raceway entrance squeaked, Grady looked expectantly for cars to roar onto the track. But they never did.

As the years rolled by, the asphalt began to crack. Weeds grew over the track. The stadium seats fell into disrepair. It seemed this was where Grady would end.

But then one day…Samantha showed up.

She was older now, the lines on her face mirroring the lines on the track. Samantha was wealthy now too. Her passion for driving, though, was steering in a different direction. And she needed Grady Grand Prix's help one more time.

Within months "Grady Go-Go-Karts" was open for business. With top-of-the line go-karts, gourmet refreshments, an arcade and water park, the venue was an entertainment destination….by invitation only. No one ever paid to get in and the only ones who did get in were the under served, disadvantaged, and disabled youths who wanted the thrill of doing the things other kids did .

Grady had to have a lot of patience. A lot of the kids, frankly, weren't very good drivers. They halted and sped up seemingly at random; crashed into the bumpers and barriers a lot. Perhaps none of them would ever turn Grady back into a big time, professional racetrack. But they all laughed a lot and had fun.

And Grady couldn't be happier.

THE END

Inspired by ATARI BYTES episode 170: GRAND PRIX

WEENA: WARRIOR PRINCESS

Weena sat in the Morlock cave. Again. And she was sleepy. Her lumpy, shuffling, glowing-eyed captor had been morlock-splaining how society works for the past half hour.

As the morlock launched into a tirade about the complexities of the morlock chain of command – which a simple *eloi* could never be expected to understand - Weena wondered if throwing herself off the top of the weird sphinx monument thing they built might not be such a bad idea. What was that thing for, anyway?

Weena considered pointing out the morlock's misstatement when he identified Kergil as the ruler who in the third age ushered in the era of eloi subjugation, not Lenigon as one of the few remaining books in that dusty old room they called a library stated. But she just didn't feel like it.

Weena had played the part of docile sheep for so long, it was a little disturbing how easy it came to her. It was like putting on a pair of pants that fit, but reminded you of the fact that you were cattle even if the color was quite flattering. Similes, Weena realized, were not an eloi strong suit.

As the morlock droned on, Weena wondered what the time traveler was doing.

He was way nicer than a morlock, and so different. No, not completely different. He wasn't as hairy as the morlock, but she could see similarities. Where the morlock thought she needed to be eaten, the traveler thought she needed to be saved. And they both primarily spoke to her in speeches and instructions; even if the morlock's speeches were more on the grunting side of things.

At this moment, Weena could hear a ruckus in the catacombs. The morlock were riled up; running and screeching. A bunch of them headed out to see what was happening. But Weena already knew. "Oh, boy," she said, eyes rolling, "I'm about to be saved."

Weena heard a lot of running and shooting. It seemed to Weena that whatever time in history the traveler came from, he was really good at such things. She wondered if she really should have wasted all those pretty flowers she stuck in the traveler's pockets.

One of the morlocks returned, eyes glowing with panic. He grunted at another one and they both waved to still more morlocks to follow; each one larger and smellier than the last. The traveler surely had his hands full. Pretentious though he could be, Weena really did like him. And it was flattering how hard he was working to impress her. His weird "time machine levers" and ancient books weren't going to stop him getting his tweed-covered backside handed to him.

The traveler might take down a few smelly morlock, but he didn't stand a chance of winning this fight.

Maybe there was something Weena could do…

While the morlocks were huddled in a corner conferring about which one would be next to face the traveler – except Barney, who really just wanted to gossip about Reginald – Weena slowly stood and quickly slipped out of her simple peasant garb. Underneath she wore only…well, actually she had on a full ninja outfit. But don't ask where she was hiding the quarter staff.

The Morlocks…well, they're powerful and aggressive, but with all that lumpy furriness they aren't the most agile and those glowing eyes offer terrible peripheral vision. Weena pounded three of them into submission before the morlocks knew what hit them.

"What is this?" one of the morlocks cried.

"I'm your worst nightmare," Weena said. "A girl with a

big stick."

She smacked another morlock upside the head. "Can you handle it?"

Some of the wimpier morlocks fled into the catacombs. That was all right. The Time Traveler could handle them. Weena focused on the stronger ones, hoping to take some of the pressure off the traveler.

Dodge, thrust, parry THWACK! On and on, Weena laid waste to the elite Morlock Guard, banshee screaming the whole time. As she dented the last one's head but good, the time traveler burst into the room, sweaty and with bow tie all akimbo. Weena quickly kicked the staff to the side.

"Weena, darling," he said. "I've come to save you." He glanced around the room. "Ah. I see some of my victims fled here to lick their wounds. Jolly good. I hope they didn't harass you too awfully."

Weena assumed the demure pose expected of the eloi. Like a child, she held out a pretty flower to the traveler, though who the hell knows where she got it.

The traveler smiled and stepped forward to accept

the gift. Over the traveler's right shoulder, Weena saw a morlock rise up, preparing to bash in the traveler's head with a rock. As the traveler closed his eyes and inhaled the flower scent, Weena snatched up the staff and thrust it into the Morlock's chest, skewering him, and shoving the dead beast to the side.

A noxious order erupted from the gaping wound. The confused traveler wrinkled his nose. "My dear, the flora here yields many surprises."

Weena giggled in stereotypical eloi, shaking her head in faux confusion. The traveler laughed. "Oh, Weena," he said. "So innocent."

The traveler and Weena embraced. Over the traveler's shoulder, Weena made the "I'm watching you," gesture at a panicked Morlock who quickly shuffled from the room.

"I must go back to my own time soon," the traveler said, sadly. "Just for a little while, but, still, how will you manage?"

Weena shrugged. "Oh, I suppose I'll get by."

Inspired by ATARI BYTES episode 171: T:ME SALVO. Also, I borrowed heaviliy from one of my favorite movies: "The Time Machine" with Rod Taylor, 1960. Thanks for that!

BAD POETRY CORNER:

BUGS: A POEM

They say 10 quintillion of you skitter across the globe

For every human, that's 200 million

The mere sight of you creates fear in our frontal lobe

But perhaps we should think twice before we kill one.

Despite all the insect fear, we still say "cute as a bug".

Why is there such a division?

Why grossed out by antennae, wings, and the thoraxes which those legs lug?

If we claim "bug" as nickname cute, we must make a decision.

So consider Bugsy Malone.

A musical film spoofing gangsters.

Sure, bugs in the name, but lighter in tone.

Quite a conundrum for the bug haters.

Meanwhile, mobster Bugsy Siegle is infamous and feared.

Without him there'd be no Las Vegas strip.

That town of gambling where food is cheap and Wayne Newton cheered.

All I can say to that is: road trip!

And now consider the case of Bugs Meany

The Tigers gang leader and foil to Encyclopedia Brown.

Indeed, he's called "Bugs" and is a town bully.

But he always loses so mark this one down.

So, finally, consider the biggest Bugs of them all.

He's mischievous, a wise guy and so very funny.

He sows chaos and laughs as victims all fall.

Perhaps no one bugs others as much as the bunny.

Where does this leave us?

Are bugs just a name or a menace?

Well, maybe it's not worth the fuss.

But it's still gross to find one in the lettuce.

Inspired by ATARI BYTES episode 172: BUGS. It would be weird if the game was actually about horse racing or something, wouldn't it?

MAXIMUM DEPTH CHARGE:

A STEVE STETSON, 1980 SUPERSPY,

ADVENTURE

The crew of the nuclear submarine the USS Nemo, froze; some holding their breath. The captain had ordered silent running. Not a sound could be heard, not even the engines. Any noise could reveal their position to the enemy that could be conning them.

There was that noise again. Captain Jelico remained stoic, though his heart beat so fast, he was sure the thumping would give them away.

Wait... Jelico realized what it was. This was impossible, but was something knocking on the outside of the sub? Had they hit something? Coral reef? Passing whale? What was it?

The crew was horrified to hear the heavy metal scrape

as the hatch thudded open, then closed again. That was impossible! They were deep underwater. No one could open a hatch in those conditions. And yet…

Heavy footfalls approached the bridge.

At a nod from Captain Jelico, the bridge crew silently drew their sidearms. It was dangerous to fire weapons in such a confined space, but these were dangerous times. Something was headed their way that shouldn't be.

The footsteps were closer now. Jelico raised his gun…

"Hello," said the beaming face that appeared in the doorway. The man removed his face mask. "Steve Stetson," he said. "Permission to come aboard? Your destroyer is about to be sunk. But I've brought the ultimate battleship. My brain."

No one spoke

"Now then," Stetson said. "Where can I throw up?"

Imagine glorious theme music here.

"Who the devil are you?" Jelico said, the gun still trained on Stetson.

"Devilish, perhaps," Stetson said. "Or so I've been told. But not the *actual* devil." Stetson's diving fins smacked wetly across the deck. Every gun in the room followed him.

"We've been investigating unusual activity in these waters," Stetson said. "Commander Maddie Grimm should have forwarded my clearance to you. They wanted to helicopter me in, but my stuff looks amazing in this wetsuit."

"I don't know who you are or what you're talking about," Jelico said.

A lieutenant handed Jelico a piece of paper. He grimaced at the newly arrived orders. "Dammit," he said. "Stand down, everyone." The crew lowered their guns.

"Still want to throw me in the brig," Stetson said. "Make me walk the plank perhaps?"

Jelico's face seemed to fold in on itself. The desk job at Quantico was looking better all the time. "You're bugging me already. Don't tempt me."

Stetson shrugged. Like that was the first time he'd heard that today.

He lowered the zipper of his wetsuit and stepped out of it, then smoothed lapels of his tuxedo and straightened his tie. He paused, picturing the roll of word-of-the-day toilet paper in the main floor bathroom of his condo, then said, "You don't have a…haberdashery… on board, do you?" I like this shirt okay, but I'm really in the mood for cuff links."

"You said you had information about who is attacking our destroyers?"

"Actually, I said your destroyer is about to be sunk," Stetson said. "As it happens, I have a pretty good idea where the enemy are. Is? Yes, where the enemy IS."

"How could you possibly know that when the entire Navy can't even figure that out?" Captain Jelico said.

Stetson grinned. "YOU just got to look around, Admiral," he said. "Me, I keep my periscope up all the time." Stetson winked at a red-headed lieutenant standing near the sub's periscope. She flipped him the bird. It was hugely unprofessional and Jelico should have reprimanded her, but, really, Stetson had it coming.

Stetson was unfazed. "So, how do we pinpoint where they are?"

"Ping them with sonar," an ensign called from the back of the room.

"Booorrrinnnngggg," Stetson said. "I've got something more fun…ready?"

All the officers glanced around, nonplussed.

"REVERSE DEPTH CHARGES!"

"That's not a thing," Jelico said. "Now, really, Stetson, we've got – "

Stetson interrupted. "You mean it's not a thing *yet*."

The ensign from earlier – Collins or Collingworth or Collington or something – called out – seriously where was he sitting? – "A depth charge destroys subs by being dropped into the water and detonating near the sub. The hydraulic shock destroys the sub. If we release a depth charge, we're dead…sir."

"Ah, that might be true, my invisible friend," Stetson said. "But I said a *reverse* depth charge. We're going to use our sub to send a depth charge in reverse to unmask the enemy so that your destroyer can, well, destroy it."

Jelico pinched the bridge of his nose, the way people do in stories to indicate weary frustration. "How, exactly, do we do that?" he asked.

"Well," Stetson said. "While I was outside, I too the liberty of…" he paused to recall a sheet of the word-of-the-day toilet paper from that night after the burrito. "…took the liberty of affixing a rather large rubber band to the sonar sphere on the nose of the submarine."

Jelico's head might have been a depth charge itself on it seemed about to explode. "What?" he managed to ask with miraculous restraint.

"It kind of looks like a stringy, sinus condition booger," Stetson observed. "Anyway. When the destroyer above us sets off a depth charge, the rubber band will catch it, stretch back and…zoom! The rubber band will fling that sucker back to the surface where it will detonate. The resulting flash will illuminate the water around us just long enough to reveal our enemy attacker. Easy-peasy."

Jelico blinked. Once. Twice. He was just about to speak when the disembodied ensign shouted, "That's stupid."

Captain," Lieutenant Lester said. "The destroyer Atari is about to launch a depth charge."

Stetson pumped his fist. "We're about to find out just how stupid. Er…inspired. Get ready, everyone."

The charge launched. Jelico braced, wondered what it would be like to spend the rest of his career scraping barnacles off the hulls of ships in dock.

The rubber band, though, did exactly as required. It caught the depth charge and flung it away like last year's regrets. And then….

Nothing.

No explosion. No nothing.

"Well, Stetson said. "That's disappointing."

The mystery ensign suddenly appeared, wrenching the headphones from his ears. "Captain," he shouted, "I've got something. A sub maybe."

"Up periscope," Jelico said.

"Yeasssss," Stetson said, grinning. "It is."

"I've got visual," Jelico said. "Arm the…"

"No time," Lieutenant Lester said.

"Prepare for ramming speed," Stetson said.

"That's not a thing," Jelico said.

"I know, but I'm betting the other sub doesn't," Stetson said. "Do it, Lieutenant."

"Belay that order, Lieutenant."

"This is so Star Trek-y," Stetson said.

"Enemy depth charge incoming, Captain," Lester said.

"Ideas?" Jelico said.

Stetson shrugged.

But then, proving – as if it needed proving – that what goes up must come down, the rubber band-launched depth charge fell back into the ocean again, intercepting the enemy charge. The two depth charges neutralized each other in a harmless undersea explosion… except for all the sea life, but, you know, whatever.

"Well, General," Stetson said to Jelico, "that all worked out well, didn't it? Now whaddaya say we sail into port and fill our portholes?"

And that was how Stetson soon found himself floating out to sea alone in a rubber life raft. He considered filing a formal complaint, if he survived. But as part of the deal when signing up with the clandestine government agency he worked for, he no longer officially existed. So it probably wasn't a court martial offense for Jelico to boot Stetson of the sub.

Stetson floated for a while, singing bawdy sea shanties to himself, until finally his superior officer Maddie Grimm floated by on a sea turtle in a fur-lined bikini. Maddie, not the turtle.

"Commander Stetson," Grimm said, formally.

"Maddie," Stetson said.

Maddie Grimm stared out over the endless expanse of ocean, patted Telly the Turtle on the head, then looked at Stetson and said, "You're an idiot."

QUEUE MAGNIFICENT END THEME

Inspired by ATARI BYTES episode 173: SUB SCAN. And more than a little STAR TREK, frankly.

GOOD ENOUGH

The door to Soundstage 17 banged first into the exterior wall as it opened, then again into the frame as the hydraulics pulled it closed. The sound reverberated off the set of children's morning show "Colonel Pop Pop" and the stunned cast and crew scattered about.

Every weekday morning, the show's star, Leslie "Skip" Roberts, had hosted "Colonel Pop Pop" in the title role since August 10, 1953. The show began as a local production and blossomed into a national favorite, unrivaled in popularity…until, ugh, *Sesame Street* came along.

The Colonel had just been informed this morning that the beloved pre-school fixture would be ending its run one month from now, May 20, 1977.

"Goddammit," Colonel Pop Pop shouted, stomping down the hall to his dressing room, fighting back tears as he removed the glued-on mustache, a replica of the one he'd worn since the beginning of the show until he'd shaved it off a couple years ago; a scorched Earth defense against grey hair. If It really bothered him, he could have just dyed the grey away, the makeup department told him, but the Colonel somehow thought that was deceitful to the children in a way a fake mustache was not.

When Randy Tompkins arrived to work that morning, he knew none of this. Randy was twenty-one and had loved Colonel Pop Pop his whole life. The Colonel was in his earliest black & white memories. When the other kids were playing baseball, he was in his basement sewing felt and ping pong balls into puppets. When the other high school kids were dating and going to the drive-in, Randy was auditioning for every community theatre production he could. When he wasn't doing that, he was studying magic or drawing monsters and cartoon animals in his sketch book or trying his hand at making films with a super eight camera.

Randy loved Colonel Pop Pop. When the studio had advertised for an intern to help out on production of the roster of local shows, Randy peed himself. Seriously. Dude had to change his pants before he got on his bike and rode to the studio to apply. The application process was rigorous. Here's how it went:

RANDY: HelloI'msuperexcitedtoapplyforthejobIoveTVsomuchandColonelPopPopinparticularhasbeenveryimportanttomeIcan'twaittodevelopmyskillsand learntomakemyown showssomeday.

ASSISTANT STUDIO MANAGER: You're hired, kid. Here's a broom.

Randy swept floors, got coffee, and ran errands. He scrubbed bathrooms after frequent office parties and fetched bourbon for the noon news anchors. He discretely diverted away any visitors to the station when the general manager was "in a conference" with David from the sales department. Before long, Randy had done everything you could do at the station (except David, who was up for it). The only job Randy hadn't tried was on-air talent.

Then Magic Millie died.

From day one of the "Colonel Pop Pop" show, Magic Millie had been a fixture. Every day, she appeared on the show. Some days, she introduced the "Good Manners for Good People" segment. Sometimes it was about saying "please" and "thank you". Sometimes it was about writing thank you letters or how to answer the telephone or holding a chair out for a lady. Other days, she appeared in skits with Colonel Pop Pop, where she imparted some sort of lesson about patience or science or kindness to the Colonel or one of the puppets. The skits usually ended with Colonel Pop Pop saying, "Gosh, you're right again, Magic Millie." Still other days, she did magic tricks for a llama and penguin puppet that lived in the fictional, vaguely military fort that housed Colonel Pop Pop and his crew.

With Millie's passing, the producers had a big hole to fill in the show. Randy convinced Colonel Pop Pop to watch the short film Randy had been working on, "Fearless Freckles" in which a bunch of animated cartoon kids with freckles stand up to neighborhood bullies.

"What do you think, Col…I mean, Leslie?" Randy still had a hard time calling Colonel Pop Pop by his real name.

"It's garbage, kid," the Colonel said, but in the kindest tone ever.

Still, though the producers agreed the film was bad, they liked Randy's exuberance and developed a new character to replace Magic Mille: BODY BOB.

The plan was each week, Body Bob would appear on the show dressed as a different body part and either talk about or show a short film about that body part. The idea was to illustrate common kid questions: why does hair grow? Why do we have fingernails? Why are Auntie Carol's boobs bigger than Mommy's? Okay, that last one came at the end of a long brainstorming session and was scrapped.

Today on the show, the day Colonel Pop Pop got cancelled, was to be the debut of BODY BOB. Randy showed up on set wearing a giant tooth costume. His first film on the show was going to be "Plaque Attack" and it was about the scourge of plaque and tooth decay. It was filled with exciting Star Wars type laser battles as the hero blasted laser-like toothpaste at the evil plaque.

Randy got the cancellation news two minutes before the camera was turned on him. Although Body Bob's eyes were filled with tears throughout his segment, it went off without a hitch.

So flawlessly, in fact, the network reran the film on the show. Every day. For the entire last month Colonel Pop Pop was a thing you could see on TV. They didn't want to pay to produce any more Body Bob films so they kept just the one. On the days that Leslie Roberts…called in "sick" during that last month, Randy even got to guest host….in costume as Body Bob in giant tooth helmet and white leotard or sometimes wearing a suit covered with plastic molds of internal organs.

When the studio finally went dark after the last episode aired, Leslie Roberts went into seclusion, sometimes rumored to be studying with Tibetan monks and other times rumored to have shaved his head and helped pioneer the underground thrash metal movement.

Randy pitched the idea of a new Body Bob show, but the studio didn't bite. It was cheaper to take whatever content the network sent than for the studio to produce its own.

None of the other local studios wanted Randy either. They all had their own version of Body Bob. Or they didn't want one. Randy offered himself as a writer, production assistant, the guy that mops up after network fight night. Nothing.

Randy had a brief gig doing commercials as Tooth Man in ads for local dentists. He couldn't wear the Body Bob costume because the network owned it, so he dressed all in white and called it good. He made good money posing with awkward-looking, smiling orthodontists and occasionally a patient. The gig came to an end the day Billy Mulligan proved the strength of his new chompers by taking a chunk out of Randy's forearm.

Randy tried to start his own production company. He wrote and directed an indie film called "POPPED", which told an autobiographical tale about a rising young TV talent who is betrayed by a metaphorical evil penguin that appears in the movie in the form of a real penguin. The film debuted at the town civic center. Four people showed up. One of them was Randy. Another was his mom. The other two thought they were at the center to hear a presentation about rerouting garbage trucks for more efficient pick up. They were disappointed.

By 1984, Randy was effectively out of show business, with the exception of saying, "Gee, Colonel Pop Pop" in his best Body Bob voice occasionally when someone recognized him in the frozen food section at the grocery store.

In 1986, Randy was busted at a porn theater for indecent exposure. "What? I'm Body Bob," he sneered drunkenly as the cops hauled him away. "The body's got lots of parts to explore."

In 1991, during another stint in rehab, Randy watched an old man with blue hair, a pirate eye patch, tattoos on his entire, clean shaven face beat up one of the other residents over a "Colonel Pop Pop" inspired thermos. "That's not an officially licensed product," the blue-haired man said as he nailed the other guy in the crotch with his cane.

The guy groaned and cursed at the blue-haired man who beaned the guy in the head with the thermos. "When you speak to me, you will call me COLONEL Pop Pop, sonny boy." As security dragged the blue-haired, pirate patch man away, Randy stared, mouth agape. "Leslie?"

It was, indeed, the colonel.

When the two men finally got clean, they opened a little business renting out bounce houses and moving vans. They made a little money and made a lot of people happy. When they delivered the bounce houses, once in a while the birthday kids' dads and moms would recognize them from the old days. That was nice. It was finally good enough.

A lot of people look down on "good enough" as settling for less. But sometimes "good enough" is exactly what you need.

Inspired by ATARI BYTES episode 174: "PLAQUE AT-TACK". Not gonna lie, "Captain Kangaroo" had a big influence too. Also thermoses.

SPACE LETTERS FROM THE SPACE FRONT LINES…IN SPACE

(Ken Burns documentary style music. Maybe sort of military march-esque…)

It's August 4, 2311. The space battle rages on. The defenders struggle mightily against the invading armada. But the space armada wants its space, man, and they do not let up. The soldiers are highly trained aliens, good at moving in straight lines without stopping and occasionally shooting without asking questions first. Or after.

Some, of the armada's soldiers, though, begin to question what they are doing, then often die, after which they stop questioning. Because they are dead.

(Ken Burns documentary style music. Sad violins and what not…)

My Dearest Blorg:

It seems some days this war never ends. We march and fight. March and fight. Tentacles worn down to become smaller tentacles. But through all the suffering, I know this invasion is just and right.

Love you 'till the next regeneration,

Glantin, second blue lieutenant alien from the left

(Ken Burns documentary style music. More violins. Maybe a cello, 'cause it's manlier...)

August 31, 2311

Dear Dad:

I sit here in the cold emptiness of space, waiting for the next wave. And I think of all the stories you told me about the great battles you fought. About how Mom liked the way you regurgitated the corpses of our enemies. And I wonder: how can I live up to your legend?

Your son,

Vlastin, third orange alien in the top second column

(Ken Burns documentary style music. Even more march-ier than the other music...)

November 9, 2311

Dear Columnister:

I hope this letter finds you well. Today, my squadron will form straight rows. We will march in formation. We will shoot our lasers. For this is the way of things. Some may not understand. They are morons.

Sincerely,

Your space love monkey, Thorg

(Ken Burns documentary style music. Sort of...neutral...)

Other soldiers were more ambivalent about their role in this invasion.

(Ken Burns documentary style music. Lighter, cause this sad part will be...funnier?...)

January 3, 2312

Dear Quagon:

Fuck this. *(AUDIO: BLEEP)*

- Stammist

(Ken Burns documentary style music. This part is tense, man...)

February 21, 2312

Dear Klorn:

Holy shit *(AUDIO BLEEP)* an entire row of my friends

got disintegrated right in front of me. What the hell, man?

Also, I hear Maewin spawned recently. Give my best to the young.

- Lank

(Ken Burns documentary style music. Confidently oblivious…)

April 18, 2312

Dear Lager:

General Blonk says tomorrow the defender will shrink away from the relentless advancement of our mighty swarm. And even though thousands before us have perished and we are behaving the exact same way, WE will be successful.

I shall wave at you from my position right up front in the first wave. Until we meet again.

- Flure

Inspired by ATARI BYTES episode 175: SPACE ARMADA from "Intellivision" month on the podcast. Shout out to Ken Burns. Like Mark Twain, jazz and baseball, I am sure to be the subject of one of his documentaries one day.

GHOST HORSES

DATELINE: CAMPTOWN, PA – Early this morning, the residents of this tranquil little mountain town in northeast Pennsylvania, were awakened from their slumber by the sound of thunder.

But it wasn't thunder.

It was horses galloping through downtown Camptown. A rainbow-colored army of equines galloped around and over vehicles, upset apple carts and left poop all over everything – including Wendell Drudge. Witnesses say no one cares much about that last part as Drudge is the town jerk-wad.

In a press conference, town Sheriff Stephanie Crowder first slipped in a massive horse apple then, after righting herself, said, "At this time, we cannot confirm where the horses came from or where they've gone. We are fairly certain that they mean to run all night, and all day."

When asked by a reporter if she'd bet her money on the bob tail nag, Sheriff Crowder only responded, "Well, as a law enforcement officer I do not engage in illegal gambling…however, I would guess somebody bet on the bay."

After that press conference, Sheriff Crowder walked the streets of Camptown, listening for the sounds of hooves on the wind. She heard nothing. Stupid wind.

The next morning, the exact same thing happened again. No sooner had Camptown picked up the pieces from the first horse stampede, when another wave of mystery horses rode into town and then disappeared at the city limits. Both the bob tail nag and the bay lifted their tails on Wendel Drudge's breakfast burrito, but again, no one cared.

Sheriff Crowder called the state police. But after she described the problem, the state police officer just started singing "Wild Horses" and hung up. A call to the Department of Homeland Security went nowhere after they determined the horses couldn't be deported as illegal immigrants.

The sheriff didn't know what to do.

After five straight days of these ghost races, the sheriff tip-toed slowly through a field of horse crap to find a relatively unsullied bench to eat some beef jerky and think. Her thoughts were interrupted, though, by the soft giggling bubbling up from over her left shoulder.

Sitting on one of those mechanical plastic horses that rocks back and forth if you put a quarter in, was a rather horse-faced, well, more donkey-faced, human. It would have been less unpleasant had it been an actual person with the head of a donkey. Cruelly, but undeniably, this person was just ugly.

"Hee-haw," the person said.

Okay, so maybe it really was a donkey-human hybrid. The sheriff's hand instinctively went to her sidearm as she stood slowly. "Do I know you?" she asked.

The donkey person laughed as the plastic stallion rocked. "Hee-haw" he said. "You know what those horses are, don't you?"

"Excuse me," the sheriff said.

"Ghost horses." The donkey person sort of spit when he said it.

"Ghost horses," the sheriff repeated, looking around to see if she was being punked.

"They're looking for the racetrack," the donkey person said, "The Camptown Racetrack. It was about five miles long. You might have heard about it." Guffaws melted into hee-haws.

"That's just a song," Sheriff Crowder said.

The donkey laughed. "So is 'Baby Got Back,'" the donkey person countered. "Doesn't make it untrue." The plastic horse stopped moving. The donkey person looked sad.

"Look, Mr…" the sheriff started to say.

"In the early 19th century, there was a racetrack," the donkey person said, ignoring the opening to introduce himself. "Every week, mighty stallions gathered on the track like equine warriors of old to do battle."

"Equine warriors?" Sheriff Crowder said, not entirely

sure what "equine" meant, but not wanting to admit it.

"One day," the donkey person said, then interrupted himself, "Hey, you got another quarter?"

"I really don't think…"

"Do you want to know about your horse problem or not?" donkey person challenged.

"What the hell," Crowder said and dropped a quarter into the ride's coin slot.

Donkey person hee-hawed for a bit as he rocked, then said, "One day, all your beliefs will be challenged. Well, except for that one about crunchy peanut butter. It's weird, but believe what you want about that."

"What are you talking about?" Crowder said.

"Ever hear of the ghost horses?" Donkey Person said.

"Oh, good grief," Crowder said. She tossed a coin to the Donkey Person. "Have another ride on me. I'm out of here."

"In the 19th century," Donkey Person called after the sheriff, "they used to have races all the time in Camptown. Constantly. Everyone loved them. Especially the ladies. They made that song about it."

"I'm familiar," Crowder said, stopping despite her better judgment.

"Doo dah. Doo dah," Donkey Person said.

"I get it. Go on."

"Those horses," the Donkey Person said, "their souls won't leap the gate into horsey heaven until they are satisfied the race is run. You must help them to cross the finish line. Go and find the Ghost Horses or see Camptown buried under Hell's Horse Apples."

Sheriff Crowder regarded the wretched thing before her. Was it lying? Why would it? What was its angle? Could it be true? Was this some sort of joke that only asses – the donkey kind – find funny? What should she do?

Finally, Crowder said, "That's the stupidest thing I've ever heard." Then she walked back to her patrol car.

The Donkey Person silently watched Sheriff Crowder go, then hung its head sadly. It was out of quarters.

*****

Sheriff Crowder sat in her car. The Donkey Person was crazy. Had to be. Even the fact that there was a donkey person around was crazy. The camp town races were foot races, not horse races. They hadn't been horse races for generations. And no one really knows if there was even a real horse track back then anyway.

Also, that song might not even be based on the horse races – such as they were back then – but rather the "Camp towns" that sprang up to house transient railroad workers. Nothing to do with horses. Or donkey persons for that matter.

Thunder rumbled. The sheriff looked through the windshield into the night sky, looking for clouds, maybe some lighting. There had been no storms predicted in the weather report today.

The thunder rolled again. Crowder listened closer and realized, it wasn't thunder at all.

It was horse hooves.

Crowder climbed out of the patrol car and stepped into the street, listening intently. Where was it coming from? The alley to the east perhaps. The courtyard behind the courthouse?

The odor of horse crap assaulted Crowder's nostrils. She turned just in time as a blur of multi-colored equine overtook her from the middle of the street. She imagined herself being trampled, crushed under the powerful legs of a dozen stallions.

The horses kept coming. The sheriff gasped, braced for the end. But then, the horses came to a stop just on the other side of Crowder. They had passed through without injury. Well most of them. One of the horses – the green one – was bisected by Crowder. It didn't seem to mind. Crowder, though, jumped to the side.

"Halt. Hold up," Crowder said, just a bit too late.

The horses stamped lightly, neighing lightly. A jockey climbed lightly from the yellow horse and stepped over to Sheriff Crowder, looking up at her with a big smile. "Hey, y'all. Name's Vernon. You all know the way to Churchill Downs?" Vernon's voice sounded like it was coming from a distance, perhaps as if he was speaking to Crowder through a long tube, even though he was standing right here, shimmering like early CGI.

"Excuse me?" Crowder said, finding it hard to focus on the words coming out of the spirit's mouth.

"We're late for the Kentucky Derby," Vernon said. His fellow long-dead jockeys chuckled. "Really, really late," Vernon said.

Crowder robotically open an app on her phone and typed in "Churchill Downs", then reported, "Uh…it's six-hundred-sixty-three miles from here."

Vernon whistled. "Well, boys," he said, looking at the jockeys. "We better hoof it. We want to get there before we're old men." They all laughed at that. "Hope the horses don't get tired." More laughter.

Vernon climbed back on his horse and the horses in perfect synchronicity galloped into the ether. In moments, Crowder was alone in the middle of the street, except for a fresh pile of horse crap on her shoes. "Really?" she said. "The horses aren't corporeal, but the manure is?"

Despite the raised eyebrows from Rick her favorite bartender, Crowder spent the rest of the evening drinking mint juleps. To forget.

But she didn't forget. The scent of horse apples lingered in Sheriff Crowder's nostrils for the rest of her days, along with an intense hatred for mint juleps.

Giddyup!

Inspired by ATARI BYTES episode 176: HORSE RACING from "Intellivision" month.

SPIN IT, BOB!

Robert Gormier took a pull from a silver flask with his initials on one side and a pair of aces on the other. Over a thirty-year career, Gormier became the world's greatest croupier. He had dealt cards, shuffled chips and made - and flushed - untold fortunes from Vegas to Atlantic City, from Macau to Montecarlo.

At the World Series of Poker, Gormier had once left legendary Vegas croupier "Elvis" Joe LeVine weeping in a pile of chips, hands and arms bleeding from countless papercuts from the playing cards that flew from Gormier's table with breakneck speed. No one was more on top of whatever game he or she was running, be it craps or poker or blackjack. Whatever the stakes, whatever the table, Gormier could make the women swoon and the guys virtually orgasm with joy at the experience of playing at his table, even as Gormier (usually) took their money. Roulette had been his specialty. A cruel irony given his present station in life.

"Back in fifteen seconds," the floor manager told Gormier, signaling the commercial break was nearly over. He took one more quick swig of Jim Beam and stowed the flask under the podium. He stared at the camera trained on him, waiting for its light to turn from red to green. Red and green, like the felt top of a gaming table...

Every time they taped one of these damn episodes and Gormier stepped out onto the garish game show set, time would stop for a moment. Not that casinos weren't garish, but they were garish in a way that your favorite uncle in the polyester suit is garish – you love him anyway. While recording these game shows, Gormier would step out of time, barely hearing the audience screaming, SPIN IT, BOB", the name of the show and his unfortunate catch phrase.

As if in slow motion, Gormier made his way to the gigantic, upright roulette wheel on one corner of the set, avoiding eye contact with Becky Schmeke or Johnny Joker or whatever schmuck the producers thought would be a good victim for this episode.

"How did I get here?" Gormier would think every single episode, immediately followed by THAT memory. "Oh yeah.."

*****

Her name was Lola. She was a show girl. Seriously. She'd heard all the jokes, so save it. Lola worked the big room at the casino where Gormier held court, the one between the Sands and the most recent one of Trump's that went bankrupt. From the first moment Lola floated through the casino, a vision in feathers and sequins, Gormier was smitten. Lola was into Gormier too. She liked the way he handled his balls… on the roulette wheel, that is.

But then there was Charlie No-Knuckles.

Now, to be clear, despite having pretty much single-handedly built Las Vegas, THE MAFIA HAS NO CONNECTION TO LAS VEGAS GAMBLING. Clear? Are we good? Okay, moving on.

BUT, Charlie No-Knuckles was a shady dude. He was Lola's ex-husband and kind of scary. Given his unusual fingers, though, he could salute really well, for what that's worth.

Charlie was also good at spending Lola's money. She made pretty good coin doing her nightly show – twice on Saturdays. Charlie would beg money off his ex-wife to help him start a restaurant, or when his buddy Dicky Dickson had to get out of town quick. For some reason, Lola couldn't say no, so she had to take a second job working the cashier desk in the casino just to make ends meet.

That's how Lola and Gormier got to know each other. And they went on to "know" each other very, very well indeed.

One night after, um, depositing his chips with Lola in the cloak room, Lola clutched Gormier tight, along with a black, size 42 men's overcoat sandwiched between them, the belt of which dangled provocatively between Lola's long legs . Lola burst into tears.

"Look, I get we didn't hit the jackpot tonight. This dude's Stetson kept falling off the shelf onto my head. Very distracting," Gormier started to say, but Lola interrupted him.

"It's all over. I'm broke," Lola said. "Charlie took everything. I'm going to have to go home to Des Moines. He'll never follow me there. Charlie thinks Midwesterners are scary."

Gormier was stunned. He couldn't lose Lola. He couldn't! "How much do you need?" he asked.

"Two-hundred-forty-six thousand-nine-hundred and two dollars," Lola said, then scrunched up her face. "And forty-two cents."

"That's a weirdly specific number," Gormier said. He couldn't give it to her, though. Given tourists' love of cheap buffets, all Gormier's money was tied up in lobster futures.

Lola shrugged. "Oh…that's all right. I'll figure something out…I guess." The trench coat belt drooped forlornly.

So quickly it would frighten him when he thought of it later, Gormier concocted a plan that would get Lola her money, get Charlie No-Knuckles off her back and only require Gormier to compromise his principles, probably decimating his reputation in the process. Well, two out of three isn't bad.

Gormier rigged the roulette wheel. On a rotating cycle during each shift he worked, the third, fourth, or fifth player, or the eighth to last player depending on the shift, would fall victim. Using a trip pin operated by a small lever under the corner of the table, Gormier would cause a player's ball to bounce from red to black or from one number to another. Then he surreptitiously pocketed half of the losing player's chips. Gormier specifically asked to work a few shifts at the lower-stakes tables – to mingle with normal folks from Des Moines for a while, wink wink. It would take longer to accrue his total, but the bosses wouldn't pay as much attention.

But Gormier was a celebrity among the croupiers, so his table was always busy and it didn't take long to pocket the two-hundred-fifty thousand.

That final night over dinner, Lola was ecstatic. Gormier, though, barely touched his food. They arranged to meet Charlie No-Knuckles for drinks at a hole-in-the-wall bar on the far end of the strip where the money would be exchanged.

"Hi ya, Bob," Charlie No-Knuckles said, waving Gormier over. He was good at waving; not so much hand-shaking.

"No-Knuckles," Gormier said evenly as he sat. "Sorry about that, by the way."

Charlie No-Knuckles shrugged. "Just means I have to get more persuasive than brass knuckles."

Again, we here at *Atari Bytes* would like to stress the mob has nothing to do with modern day Vegas.

Gormier sipped the dirty martini waiting for him. Say what you want about Charlie No-Knuckles – though never to his face – he knew how to order a drink.

"You got it?" No Knuckles asked.

"I got it," Gormier said, a cold goo filling the space where his soul had been, like rust eating out the pick-up truck he'd be driving in Pig Hollow, Nowheresville after all this was over.

Lola arrived then. It was always a little jarring to see her walking around without the makeup and sequins, being just the wonderful, normal person she was.

It was even more jarring, though, when Lola sat between the two men and kissed Charlie No-Knuckles full on the mouth.

In the history of brilliant responses, Gormier's wasn't one of them.

"Uhhhhhh," Gormier said.

Lola disengaged the lip lock with a wet, sucking sound and smiled brightly. "Honey, do you have our cash?"

Gormier's heart fell into that hole his soul used to occupy. "What the…what the….?"

"Sorry," Lola said, and maybe sorta kinda meant it? Gormier wasn't sure he could read her anymore. "But when Charlie called and said he needed my help, I couldn't say no."

Charlie squeezed Lola's shoulders. "Help getting us to the French Riviera you mean." They laughed. Gormier did not.

"But…" Gormier wanted to say, "How could you?" but that would be cliché. Besides, the answer to how a woman he loved could dupe him was probably not one he wanted to hear.

"Our plane leaves in a couple hours," Lola said. "So if you wouldn't mind?"

Gormier glanced around and prepared to hand over

life as he knew it. As soon as he passed to Lola the Macy's shopping bag full of cash, the FBI agents moved in.

As the agents lead away a smirking Charlie No-Knuckles – they didn't bother with handcuffs, since the no-knuckles thing made it easy to slip out of them. They just quickly hustled Charlie into a waiting black SUV.

Lola, in tears, asked Gormier, "How could you?"

Man, this was hard. Gormier almost broke then, but he held it together with a shrug. "What happens in Vegas…can get you five to ten in the state pen."

For his cooperation, Gormier only did six months in a low security prison. His croupier career was over, but he got a deal to write a book that did moderately well and he lived off the advance he got for a while.

And then the TV producers came.

"You seriously want to put me on a loud, brightly colored set, giving money to tourists who think they're going to get rich?"

"How is that different than what you did at the casinos?"

"Well, I don't know…" Gormier hedged.

"We'll give you a cut of the syndication rights."

"Where do I sign?"

So when Becky Schmecky – or whatever – stood quivering with anticipation on that game show set, Gormier tried real hard to remember his cut of the syndication rights.

"Becky," Gormer began.

"Eileen," the contestant corrected.

"Whatever," Gormier said, trying to laugh it off "Now Evelyn," he resumed. "You have four hundred dollars on the line. There are thirty-five numbers on the roulette wheel. You correctly answered all the questions in our astrophysics lightning round, so you have five "bets" you can make. Now, you can place those individually, or you can split your bets and maybe double your money. All or nothing, Esther. What's it gonna be?"

Eileen place her markers on 1, 10, 19, 31 and 32. She had personally significant reasons for each number which she explained in excruciating detail, but Gormier tuned it out. "Ellen," he said. "should we see if lady luck is in the house?"

"SPIN THAT WHEEL, BOB!" Eileen shouted.

The audience parroted the catch phrase back. The already meager light within that kept Gormier going flickered a little. The little hole in Gormier's soul had closed some since Lola betrayed him. Now, it was just big enough for the tennis-ball-sized ball in the show's fake roulette wheel. The soul hole, now, for all Gormier knew, was filled with his enlarged liver. Whatever gets you through the day.

Eileen cheered. The ball dropped. Eileen cheered some more in slo-mo, dream-state, distorted audio. Gormier pictured tiny show girls plastering a smile onto his stupid face.

SPIN IT, BOB ran for ten seasons. After that, Gormier did one season stints on "Card Cut-Ups", "Poker-Ace", and "You Bet-cha!" Then he retired to a ranch in Montana, never once setting eyes on a cow.

Inspired by ATARI BYTES episode 177: ROULETTE, from Intellivision month.

BAD POETRY CORNER:
DEADLOCKED

I'm a thief, running through the night.
Searching for a victim.
I firmly believe my cause is right.
People exist for me to trick 'em.

Nowhere to rest, not a moment to lose.
Constantly chased, be it cops or loves lost.
This door is locked, that one is too.
I never stay in one place, but at what cost?

Why, you ask, why do I do it; this life of crime?
Well, what other life is there?
I made my choices. There's no time.
I could make excuses, but they won't care.

I could have been a cop, you know.
But money is a siren call.
Life is a river with unpredictable flow.
But cash buys access to all.

No Robin Hood am I. No peasants cheer.
What I take is for me alone.
What's yours is mine, that I hold dear.
My reputation has only grown.

The banks all know me, but I don't fear.
Cathy knew me too.
My infamy is a fine story to hear.
But not to my Cathy Lou.

Another narrow escape.
This escapade is through.
This life to some is a mere jape.
But it's the only life I ever knew.

Inspired by ATARI BYTES episode 178: LOCK 'N' CHASE, Intellivision Month.

BAD POETRY CORNER:
LOG ROLLIN'

He's a jungle man, loves adventure

Loves danger and alligators too

He's a good man, who's crazy 'bout vine jumpin'

Loves scorpions and the jungle too

But it's a long day, he's tired from running.

There's lots of logs rollin' through the swamp

And I'm a bad travel agent, 'cause I misled him

I'm a bad agent for dupin' this chump

Now I'm not free

Log rollin'

Yeah I'm not free

Log rollin'

Now all the scorpions walkin' through the tunnels

Move super slow toward the next ladder

And all the scorpions are waiting in the shadows

And my weary clients are left with crappy trips

Now I'm not free

Log rollin'

Yeah, I'm not free

Log rollin'

Log rollin', now I'm log rollin, now I'm

Log rollin', now I'm log rollin, now

I wanna go down, sprint over the quicksand

I wanna show him all of the treasures

But as for a refund, not gonna give him nothin'

I need cash, yo. No one uses travel agents now…

Now I'm rollin (Log rollin, now I'm log rollin, now)

Inspired by ATARI BYTES episode 179: PITFALL! From Intellivision Month and the late, great Tom Petty, whose estate, I hope, is forgiving.

ROSIE THE RIVETER…OF DEATH!

Hello, again robot rooters! Tank thankers! Fans young, old, and cryogenically unfrozen! Welcome to RobotTank Stadium. I'm your commentator Earlectric Jackyouhoff. Tonight's bout promises to be one for the history books. Or at least the repair shop.

In the green corner, from every cheesy sitcom imagining of a robot ever, here is that wisecracking Screwball of Sass, Rosie Robot!

Rosie Robot, by all appearances a twenty-something woman with an enormous bow in her perfect hair glides into the arena wearing overalls. She leans stiffly out of the top of the tank, broad, never wavering smile on her face. In stilted words, she says, "I like the night life. I like to boogie. And kick butt." She blinks in time to her own words.

On television screens at home, over melodramatic music, we see a large house on a quiet street. In voice-over, we hear Rosie, still speaking in the same stilted speech:

"I arrived at the Gleason residence just when they needed me most."

We see the Gleason's living room. Two precocious children are gleefully ransacking the place – books all over the place, an overturned flower pot, pizza on the cat – as the detached dad sits reading one of the newspapers; at least until the boy cuts the paper in half with gardening shears.

Mrs. Gleason enters the living room and throws up her hands in overacted sitcom fashion. "This place is a zoo, I tell you," she says.

The kids make animal noises. (Laughtrack)

"Whatever are we going to do?" Mrs. Gleason says.

"Already on it, Gladys," Mr. Gleason says.

The doorbell rings. Mrs. Gleason answers it and an ethnic stereotype in coveralls wheels in a large box – just about human-sized actually. Mr. Gleason stiffs him on the tip and he exits.

"What is it, dear?" Mrs. Gleason says.

"Salvation," Mr. Gleason answers.

"Like when Daddy doesn't order a second bean burrito," the girl kid mugs to the camera. (Laugh track)

In comedic fashion, the Gleasons manage to get the box open. At first, there is stunned silence. And then, Roberta steps out, the huge smile already in place. She is wearing the trademark large bow in her hair and a traditional black and white maid's uniform.

"It's a girl," boy kid says.

"No kidding, doofus," girl kid says. (Laughtrack)

"Girls by mail," the dad says. "I love the postal service."

Laughtrack.

In voice over, Rosie describes a series of whacky sitcom adventures. It was a good life – although she's a robot – but since she never ages, eventually the Gleasons got old and died, so Roberta buried them in the backyard next to the four goldfish and some sort of slug thing buried previously.

Rosie plays an audio clip of someone crying in an effort to convey emotion. "The world outside the Gleason's yard was a hellish landscape," she says. "I mean, it was 2019 after all. Every robot for itself. Well, except the Mix 'n' Max Bots. They have interchangeable parts." She grins at the camera. "I have my friend Steve's teeth." The giggling is unsettling.

Rosie explains that she learned to fight from her run-ins with the biker gangs – sentient motorcycle cyborgs. Somehow, she managed to overcome this bleak period and found herself in THE TANK, robot-kind's premiere combat arena.

The announcer puts on a serious face – he keeps it in a drawer along with the frowny face, the smiley face and the "oh my god that stinks" face. Each one attaches with a hex wrench that's usually hard to find, but fortunately it was available tonight.

"Rosie," the announcer says. "Your story is compelling and heart-wrenching."

Rosie hands the announcer a hex wrench. The announcer politely declines.

"What would winning in Robot Tank mean to you?" the announcer asks.

Rosie takes a deep breath, which is weird since she's a robot.

"What would it mean?" she says. "Seriously? Does not compute. I do noooootttt…" And then Rosie collapses because her battery died.

"Well, while Rosie recharges her battery pack, let's hear from your challenger. In the red corner, welcome DeathMetal."

Clouds hover over the Robot Tank. An ominous fog rolls in. From its center, a monolith emerges and towers over the announcer.

"Welcome to the Tank, DeathMetal," the announcer says.

Oppressive silence.

The announcer hex screws on his no-face face because, frankly, DeathMetal is a little scary. "DeathMetal," he says. "What would victory in the Tank today mean to you?"

More of that oppressive silence, but then a tiny door opens in DeathMetal's ankle, out of which a little wind-up toy mouse, no more than a few inches tall, marches out. The mouse looks into the camera, which has followed it to the floor. The mouse squeaks, "Look into my eyes. Deeply."

The viewing audience does that, its collective senses assaulted by scenes of torment and carnage so vicious, their souls ache from the strain.

It's all over in a matter of seconds.

The wind-up mouse leaves a single red rose on the battlefield and marches back inside DeathMetal.

The announcer turns to the camera. "Well, with that, I think it's time to set the stage for today's epic contest. Rosie Robot versus DeathMetal. Moments from now –"

The announcer is interrupted as Rosie leaps up, fully charged. "Oh, yeah. It is on, be-atch!" She pauses. "Sorry. Sorry."

The stadium – the tank – is suddenly silent. The two robotic warriors face off from opposite ends of the arena.

DeathMetal brandishes a titanium buzz saw. Rosie the Robot brandishes an innocent looking daisy which can snap out whip-like tentacles of electrified thorns.

The referee is a device that sort of looks like a cross between a 1980s style boom box and a goat. BoomGoat calls for the battle to start and then…

Billy wakes up. The boy sits upright in bed, impossibly blue eyes blinking in the confusion of newly regained consciousness. He tries to remember what he just dreamed. Robot Tank? It was so silly.

Billy can't imagine a world of walking, talking robots, living independent lives, let alone fighting each other. Don't people fight enough on their own? Why would their robots fight too? By choice even? What kind of world would that be?

Billy clears his mind of such thoughts. He leaps from his bed and marches out of the room to begin his day. As he leaves the sleep chamber, the charger cord detaches from the wall and auto-recoils neatly into android Billy's left thigh, the little compartment sealing itself tightly.

Inspired by ATARI BYTES episode 180: ROBOT TANK.

TURN LEFT! NO RIGHT! NO LEFT!

Missy Packelmann flopped down on the couch, the daily grind still chattering about in the recent past, but unable to touch her here in the present. Kicking off her shoes, she stared absently at her phone. A bunch of Twitter responses to some dumb thing she posted that morning that she couldn't even remember now. Several people liked the cat-related meme on Facebook. Oh, look, a text from Iris:

"M," the text said. "Half-priced margaritas. You in?"

No, No, Missy was not. Unless Dabney's was delivering alcohol now – not a bad thought – Missy was *out*. She wasn't going anywhere because that would require putting on shoes. And pants. And probably constricting undergarments.

A text from Brenda: "So are you doing the fair on Saturday?"

Oh, god, that stupid – sorry, *community revitalizing* – fundraiser she's agreed to work on this weekend. Missy had promised to bring cupcakes – homemade, not store bought – and set up tables and check people in and what not. On a Saturday. After the work week at a place adjacent to Hell where all the men wore sweat stains and arrogance strangled but not killed by bad ties, and all the women were that kind of angry where people pretend not to be angry, but obviously are, so that not only are you worried about what they're angry at, you're annoyed that they won't just get on with being angry so that this bit of the work day can just be over already.

Missy pressed the chilled beer can against her forehead. Her phone chimed again. Another text. Sue this time. Sue just liked to text to tell Missy about the latest non-adventure in her life.

"He called again," the text read.

"Barry?" Missy typed back, knowing for certain it was.

"Yeah. I didn't answer him," Sue wrote.

"Cool." Then Missy typed. "Gotta go. The cupcakes are on fire." It was a little rude, Missy knew, but she already knew what Sue's next text would have been. Something about how Barry called again and she caved and bought the life insurance. Barry was Brenda's life insurance agent and had Sue in his sights for his next client.

*****

The next morning, it all started again. Six a.m. alarm. Cold shower – she really needed a new water heater. Cupcakes from last week's baking adventure for breakfast – one, then two, then three. She gobbled them like power pellets from that video game her brother liked when they were kids.

Missy's cubicle was the third one left of the rear entrance door to the office complex. This meant that all day long she could hear the metal door bang open, then close as co-workers went in and out getting sodas and coffee before winding their way through the maze of cubicles.

Brenda stopped by Missy's cubicle mid-morning. Brenda worked in purchasing, but seemed to spend most of her time in Missy's department, accounts receivable. "Cupcake update?" she said, by way of greeting.

"Baked half of them last night," Missy lied.

"Cool," Brenda said and was gone. Brenda was a good friend, even though she lacked social niceties.

Iris wandered in. She was a supervisor in marketing. She had her own office with a door, which was good because she was often hung-over.

"I know I'm not your boss," Iris said.

"Uh-oh," Missy responded.

"But you are ordered to come out with me tomorrow night. Dabneys has free wings."

"I'm baking cupcakes tomorrow night."

Iris made a face. "The fund raiser?"

"The fund raiser."

"It's not even one of the good charities," Iris objected.

Missy shrugged. "I should probably get some work done."

Iris returned the shrug and disappeared.

A short time later, Penelope appeared in the cubicle open space where the door should be. Missy really wished she had a door. Also, she wished that she had made more friends outside of work.

"Did you hear?" Penelope said. "Cherie is in the office."

Missy froze. Seriously? Cherie Strawberry was the assistant to the regional administrative director liaison to the vice-president. It was well known that the VP's office was looking for a new deputy to all that other stuff. Cherie was probably in the office today scouting out the talent.

Missy had to make sure Cherie knew that she, Missy,

was that talent.

"Where is she?" Missy asked.

"Other end." Penelope pointed. "She was showing Clifton how to upload the monthly data summary analysis report encapsulation."

Missy stood on tippy-toes to peer over the cubicles. Cherie was quite tall and she was clearly visible across the maze of cubicles. Missy was determined to accidentally on purpose run into her so she could charm her with a firm handshake and some very useful off-the-cuff facts she diligently memorized for the sole purpose of wowing Cherie. Now Missy just had to recall some. "Excuse me, P," Missy said. "I have a date with destiny." She set out.

"I dated Destiny last month," Penelope muttered. "Made me pick up the check every time."

Missy weaved in and out of the cubicles. There was no destination in this office, physically or professionally, that was a straight line. Missy's OCD kicked in and she felt compelled at each cubicle she passed to turn the little circular "In or Out" sign everyone had, but most ignored, to in or out depending on what was appropriate.

Cherie was on the move. She went from Clifton's cube, left to Becky's and down the row to Jeff's cube. Jeff apparently showed Cherie something funny because she laughed; or she was just being polite.

Missy took a shortcut through the quiet section where some of the cubicles held old office equipment. There were three cubicles, though, where the occupants were having a heated discussion…about cookies.

Missy tried to briskly walk past. Maggie, Wayne and Joaquin, though each held out a hand holding a different flavor cookie. "Tell them mine is better," Maggie said.

"No, mine," Wayne said.

"They're both morons," Joaquin countered. "Coconut all the way."

Missy snatched the cookies, one after another, and devoured the little discs.

"Mmm, all good," Missy said, spraying chocolate chips and the aforementioned coconut as she kept moving.

Missy could hear Cherie. She was right around this next corner, telling Reggie about the soon to be announced revisions to the office procedure manual. Missy was almost there. The prize was nearly hers!

Missy's phone chirped. Text. It was Sue.

"My life is over," the text read.

Dammit.

"Barry again?" Missy typed back.

"Dax," was the reply.

This was new.

"Dax who?"

"It's so bad…."

Dax who?"

"He wants to clean my gutters," Brenda explain. "Calls all the time."

"Let him," Missy typed back. "You need it."

Missy turned the phone off and shoved it back in her pocket. Intersection with Cherie Strawberry was imminent. Getting this job would be a huge life boost.

Cherie's back was turned as Missy approached. She was talking to Magna, the newest purchasing department hire. Cherie was probably putting the fear of God into her. Soon, that would be Missy's job. "Um, excuse me, Cherie?" Missy said, holding out her hand; locked and loaded.

Cherie Strawberry turned, the administrator smile wavering and regrouping. Who was this? "Oh, Missy Packelman. Hello." She took the proffered hand. Was it an enthusiastic shake? Missy couldn't tell.

"Hope I wasn't interrupting anything," Missy said.

"No, not at all," Cherie said. "I was just telling Magna she got the deputy job."

"Oh."

Inspired by ATARI BYTES episode 181: MS. PAC MAN for the Atari 7800.

HUMBLE PIE...ER, COBBLER

Mad Dog slides out one of the chairs from the dining room table and sits. The room is cool and the wooden rungs of the chair chill Mad Dog's back, prompting him to sit up straighter. "Is it on? It better be on."

Mr. Mean pouts. "I told you it was. You don't have to be mean." He double-checks that the little light on the video camera is, indeed, on.

He places another dining room chair next to Mad Dog and sits.

"Big Chief, Skin Head, come on," Mad Dog calls. "Camera's rolling."

Big Chief, topping the scales at 310, lumbers in. "Anyone want some of this?" He holds out a pan of peach cobbler.

"Not now," Mad Dog barks. "We gotta do this."

"But thank you for going to the trouble," Mr. Mean says, shooting a look at Mad Dog.

Big Chief shrugs, sets the pan on the table and places another dining room chair on the other side of Mad Dog. He sits.

Skin Head hustles in, wiping his hands on a pink apron, which he then tosses aside.

"Oh, you have some sweet potato on your mask, Skin Head," Mr. Mean says.

Skin Head wipes at his chin with a forearm. "Thanks." He sits in a fourth chair.

"All right," Mad Dog says. "We're all here." He looks directly into the camera. "To whomever is viewing this video," he says. "Let this recording be our last will and testament." He looks at the other men. "Testament, right?" They all nod. Mad Dog looks at the camera.

"On account of tomorrow…we die."

Mad Dog leans toward the camera, his massive head filling the frame. "When I was five, deep in bayou country in Louisiana, I had a dog. He was a good ol' pup named…well, Good 'Ol Pup. My cat Cat and my Norway rat named Sebastian were great, but G.O.P and me were inseparable. We went everywhere together. That is, until a gator done swallowed 'im up, collar and all. I've always hated that gator. Why am I telling you this?"

Mad Dog leans over to Mr. Mean. "Seriously," he says. "Why am I telling them this?" Mr. Mean whisper-hisses something the camera's microphone doesn't pick up. "Oh, right," Mad Dog says.

"So, anyway," Mad Dog says to the camera, "I done spent my whole life wallopin' people like they was those gators. And I'm kinda sorry 'bout that. Nothin' can bring G.O.P. back to me, but I reckon I'll be joinin' him real soon."

The other wrestlers pat Mad Dog on the back as he leans back in his chair, spent.

Big Chief slides his chair so that he is staring intently into the little LED light on the camera. It should hurt his eyes, but he doesn't blink.

"I'm from Big River, Utah," he says. "I mostly like to beat people down." He pauses, considering. Then, "I think that's pretty self-explanatory." Not sure how to close, he stands so that only his torso is in frame, says "Thank you," and sits.

There's a few seconds of Mr. Mean and Skin Head each offering to the let the other go next. Finally, Mr. Mean just starts talking.

"So, ah, not many people know that Jersey is the slime capital of the Northeast," Mr. Mean says. Turning to someone off camera, he whispers, "No, I don't want any more cobbler. Thanks." Pause. "Well, just stick it in the fridge, then." Then he looks back at the camera. "When I say 'slime', I don't mean, like, they'se bad people. The people there are actually nicer than they get credit for. Anyway, I mean when I was on the streets, the streets flowed with rivers of living slime. The media, they didn't write about that much; too busy with the Midwest Robot Marauders. Well, robots might be sexier than slime, but when twelve square yards of ooze coalesces into a gorgeous, though green, human female form and goes for your 'nads, you're not thinking about plain old sex like any other Saturday night, let me tell ya."

The other wrestlers back away a bit from the table.

"Well, you're not," Mr. Mean says, a bet defensive. "Anyway, poundin' the snot outta that walking snot is where I learned to fight. It's where I learned to live. It's where I learned to…." He side-eyes the other wrestlers. "Well, it's where I learned to love. To love rasslin. It was all I was ever meant to do. It's how I came into this world. And it's how I'll go out of it. Hand me that damn cobbler." Mr. Mean crabs a fistful of cobbler and gnaws at it.

Skin Head turns the camera on himself. He's chosen the blue leather mask this time. Mr. Mean gets his name, a bit, because he gets irritable when people assume the bald one is Skin Head and he's the one in the mask, but Skin Head wears the mask to hide his…well, not exactly shame, but sort of like shame.

"Here's the thing," Skin Head says. "I got a really ugly head. I'm from Idaho see, a state pretty much only known for three things – potatoes, being the state that might be Iowa and vice versa, and white supremacists – lots of which are called skin heads." Skin Head sighs deeply. "Only, I got my name the legit way; my first name is S.K., from my mom "Susie" and my dad "Ken". And my last name is Inhead. S.K. Inhead. I wear the mask 'cause…"

The others chuckle. "Go ahead," Mad Dog says. "Tell 'em."

"This is stupid," Skin Head says.

"Go on," Mad Dog says, sitting forward, eagerly."

"I wear the mast 'cause…it makes me feel pretty."

High fives all around…and a hug from Mad Dog.

"So, um," Mad Dog says to the camera. "I guess that's it. Tomorrow, it's one more match. We probably won't get to tell you this stuff, you know, after."

Inaudible mutterings all around the table.

"So. See ya," Mad Dog says. Somebody turns off the recorder.

*****

There was a record crowd at the title match the day after that recording. A rowdy, raucous bunch, eager for some action. Mad Dog and Big Chief were the undercard, followed by Mr. Mean and Skin Head. The action was intense. Pile drivers, headlocks, wrestlers flying off the turnbuckles.

The final bout was a tag team match up. This time, Big Chief and Mad Dog versus Mr. Mean and Skin Head. Big Chief picked up Skin Head, spun him like a homo sapien pinwheel, preparing for the body slam to beat all body slams and then…

Life-sized Hungry Hungry Hippos emerged from the four corners of the ring, devouring the wrestlers whole. How did those men know what their fate would be? Well, shoot, you might as well ask how people know professional wrestling is real. They. Just. Know.

Inspired by ATARI BYTES episode 182: TITLE MATCH PRO WRESTLING.

HELL'S CEREAL

Dax Ledderson, ace test pilot, blinked hazel eyes into the unforgiving New Mexico sun. He pulled down the zipper of his flight suit a bit and pulled out his phone. Eight-fifteen a.m. That couldn't be right. Only a moment ago, it was seven-thirty-one.

Also a moment ago, he was in an experimental aircraft

approaching Earth's upper atmosphere.

Wasn't he?

He was pretty sure.

But not *that* sure…

Ledderson wondered if he should call someone. But who? To say what? "Yeah, this is Major Dax Ledderson. Can y'all tell me if I was up in a plane this mornin'? I can't quite recollect."

The scent of chorizo and green chile breakfast burritos filled Ledderson's nostrils. His stomach growled.

He looked to his left. Nothing.

He looked to his right. The only visible structure was a ramshackle breakfast joint. Fancy that coincidence. Not that it mattered. Ledderson was starving and he'd just spotted an oasis in this desert. And it had a griddle. How he'd gotten here could wait. His stomach could not.

A rusty little bell overhead tinkled when Ledderson stepped through the restaurant door. The bell fell and rolled in a half circle before coming to rest by a newspaper box that hadn't seen a newspaper since Reagan was in office.

Ledderson stepped to the counter. As he sat, the swivel bar seat creaked a little, but there was no one else in the restaurant to disturb. Ledderson caught a glimpse of himself in the grease-smudged side of a napkin holder. A small cut on his cheek had bled into his beard, staining some of the flecks of gray. How did that get there? The cut AND the gray?

The swinging door to the kitchen opened and a pixie-ish girl of nineteen or so emerged in a waitress outfit and pristine white apron. She had a pot of coffee and a wide smile. "Mornin'," she said. "Coffee?"

"Yes, please," Ledderson said. His voice sounded familiar, but tentative, like it wasn't supposed to be heard.

The girl filled his cup. She didn't have a nametag. In his head, Ledderson called her Salem, though he wasn't sure why.

"Could I get a breakfast burrito?" Ledderson asked.

"Salem" smiled. "Well….," she said. "You could, but we

have something better."

"What's that?"

"Cereal."

"Cereal?" Ledderson repeated. "Like corn flakes?"

"Better," 'Salem' said. "It's an awesome mix of corn, rice and oats with just a bit of sugar and vanilla for flavor. Our own mix. We toast it right here in the flames below. That is, in our own specially built oven."

Ledderson frowned. "I dunno," he said. "Those burritos smell really good."

"Salem" laughed. "Oh, those aren't burritos you're smelling. It's... Anyway, can I bring you a bowl? You won't regret it."

What did he have to lose? "Load me up," he said.

"Salem" moved back toward the kitchen. Ledderson thought he noticed the slightest hitch in her step.

Moments later, she returned with the bowl of cereal. As she set it down, she craned her neck as if trying to relieve stiffness.

"I got a good chiropractor that could fix that up," Ledderson said, then looked down at the bowl. The crispy bits looked good as cereal can look. Ledderson poured some milk from the small metal decanter next to the bowl.

Salem smiled. "Nothing can help me." She held up a second bowl, this one with fruit. "Blueberries?" Salem asked. "Picked fresh."

"Please," Ledderson said.

The cereal stayed surprisingly crisp in the milk. The crunch was pleasing. Notes of vanilla and cinnamon played across Ledderson's tongue. "Hey, you're right," he said as he took another spoonful. "Not bad."

"Salem" blinked a few times, smiled and turned away. A faint whirr filled the diner's silence. "More...," 'Salem' started to say. But as the word "coffee" trembled from her tongue, she spasmed. Hot java splashed over the counter as the coffee pot hit the edge and clattered to the floor along with her right arm.

A gash tore itself in the back of "Salem's" uniform, A metallic apparatus pushed through and quickly formed itself into a wing on her right side. The left side followed suit.

Ledderson tried to scream as "Salem's" face peeled away, revealing a robot insectoid face beneath. Compound eyes regarded Ledderson with contempt. Ledderson's scream drowned in a wash of skim milk and the most amazing cereal he'd ever eaten. He just couldn't stop. He hefted the spoon even as his eyes remained locked on the creature before him.

In the next spoonful, the bits of oats were replaced with miniature flaming pumpkins. The heat seared Ledderson's lips and tongue, but it just tasted so good. He tried to stand, to run, but the short order cook – or perhaps short order dragonfly – buzzed from the kitchen and the humanoid insect held Ledderson in place. Since he couldn't move anyway, he took another spoonful. God, this stuff was good.

The two very bad bugs, but decent restaurant staff, communicated via telepathy. They nodded in agreement. In a hiss, the former "Salem" asked, "Want a second helping?"

It took every ounce of Ledderson's military training to fight the urge to say, yes, but in the end all he could mutter is, "I think I should go. What do I owe?" as he sank back down on the bar stool, waiting for the check.

"Your money's no good here," the cook said. "But there is something you can do."

Ledderson glanced down as the cereal bowl started to wobble on the counter. Cold milk splashed across the burns on his face as a clawed, beastly hand thrust out from within the bowl, grabbed Ledderson by the throat and pulled the confused patron into the depths of Hell. Ledderson never even got an after-dinner mint.

Within minutes, the diner was reset, pristine as always. "Salem," in human form once again, and with a name tag that said, "Vicki", put on a fresh pot of coffee.

A woman in hiking gear entered the diner, perched her sunglasses atop her head and asked, "Excuse me? My jeep for some reason suddenly broke down outside. Is it okay if I wait in here until roadside assistance shows up? I'm starving."

Vicki beamed. "Well, pull up a chair. We've got just the thing…"

Inspired by ATARI BYTES episode 183: FIRE FLY

BAD POETRY CORNER:
MOVING ON, STANDING STILL

I sit here in this parking lot
Surveying all the things I've got.
Or don't.

My friends jet off to parts unknown.
They laugh and giggle at photos on their phones.
I idle quietly in the corner.

So many streets we all race down.
So many avenues through life's town.
I thought I knew which way to go.

No. That's a lie I told myself.
I put my fears up on a shelf.
Don't my friends have fears?

When lights turn green, we hit the gas.
I started out great, but my friends did pass.

I didn't crash, but I didn't win either.

They found their callings; race cars, plane technicians.
One's a prize-winning mathematician.
I call my job; it doesn't call me.

But keeping all the balls in the air
Means having to grow a pair.
That's life on the streets, folks.

In life, we slalom and swish on downhill skis.
Metaphors for life are easy, you see.
But on life's tally, do the numbers add up?

Skis, planes, cars – choose your metaphor.
All life requires is for you to be a mover.
I'll do my best if you will too.

Poem crossing the finish line; might say just in time.
But you take your own time to find your road.
Life hurries enough on its own.

Inspired by ATARI BYTES episode 184: STREET RACER. And probably every office cubicle motivation poster ever.

WHY DOES EVERYONE KEEP FLASHING GORDON?

Gordon didn't know what was happening, but it was amazing.

The men and women around him were going about their business. That dude was selling hot dogs out of a cart. There was a woman over there tending to a sick koala bear. Through the bay window of a luxury townhouse, Gordon could see two women baking while a dude in a chef's hat and luxuriant mustache looked on.

It was all very ordinary mid-day stuff in Gordon's world. But then…

As Gordon watched the goings-on, a delivery man marched by, said, "Good day," and dropped his pants. The delivery man's package fell front and center. "Lovely afternoon, isn't it?" the man said and kept walking.

"Uh," Gordon muttered and averted his eyes. A dark-haired woman standing next to the open hood of a red mustang wiped her hands on her overalls and waved Gordon over.

"Hello," the woman said in an Aussie accent. "The engine's gone a bit wonky. Tires are flat. Even the electrical is all kaput." She sighed. "Could you check my headlights?" Then she stripped down to nothing, which is really not advised when working so close to a hot engine. "I think I left a screwdriver over there somewhere." Stunned and unsure where else to look, Gordon followed the woman's bum as she walked away to find it.

What in the world? Why was everyone flashing Gordon?

"Hey, kid," a deep gruff voice called. Mr. McGillicuddy ran the meat shop across the street from the autobody shop, which Gordon was keen to get away from. He was a kindly old gent, with a bark worse than his bite. In the window today, though, pork links weren't the only sausages on display in the front window. But they were definitely the freshest.

"Eww," Gordon groaned and ran down the street. As he ran, the hot dog vendor waved his wares for all to see.

Gordon had to jump into the street for safety as the veterinarian rode by Lady Godiva style, bareback on a white stallion.

The bakers from the town house shoved their cupcakes in Gordon's face and the baker dude found a new place to hang his chef's hat.

"Aahh, I gotta get out of here," Gordon screamed.

Rounding a corner, Gordon bumped into Officer Maggie, the town cop.

"Why in such a hurry?" Officer Maggie asked.

"You won't believe this," Gordon said. "All these people keep flashing me."

"Really now," Officer Maggie said, incredulous. "Let's go check this out, shall we?"

Gordon and Officer Maggie returned to the town square. The mechanic, the vet, the hot dog vendor,

Mr. McGillicuddy, they were all fully clothed. Everyone. Just doing what they do, when they're not getting naked.

Officer Maggie put hands on hips and said to the town citizens, "Excuse me," but no one responded. She cleared her throat and tried again, a little louder. Still no response.

"Try flashing your badge," Gordon said.

Officer Maggie flashed them all right. And you won't believe where the badge was.

Gordon ran, sprinting through town. All along the way, he was met with flesh, much of which was not really meant to be seen in the light of day; Earl the stable boy at the ranch; Marsha the accountant for whom the sum of her parts added up to big time nudity; Randy the baseball player who kept his balls in a sack.

All productive citizens of the town…and all fully nude.

Gordon sat back to consider what he'd seen today. A little smile crept across his features. He had to admit, he kind of… liked it. Was that wrong? Was it wrong to be naked? The human body was a totally natural thing. Was he evil for liking all of them naked? He really didn't know.

Gordon's sister Gretchen, was more certain.

"Mom," Gretchen shrieked. "Gordon took all the clothes off my dolls again. Tell him to stop."

Ten-year-old Gordon sprinted from his little sister's bedroom to go find other mischief to get into. Maybe he could knock down his brother Glen's Lego buildings. He'd just blame Gretchen for it.

And one day, far in the future, that ten-year-old-boy would grow up to be president of the United States.

Inspired by ATARI BYTES episode 186: FLASH GORDON. Never been to Australia, so not sure why the story seems to take place there. But you Australians have as much right to get naked as anyone else, I say.

BAD POETRY CORNER:
THE NATIONAL ANTHEM OF WAR

Spread there before us, behold this great land.

Power is great, if only we'll take it.

Embrace the good to be had, fear not the sad.

For the world can be bad as we wish to make it.

War is not just soldiers in battle; though that's fun as can be.

Fearing just human enemies leaves much to chance.

War is also for vaccines and climate and things hard to see.

Fight all you can; embrace the romance.

Race, sex, ethnicity. Religion too.

Hate, words, money are all great weapons.

Tired of fighting? Push on through.

Be super loud and they'll listen to us.

Sure, we sound obnoxious and hateful; like it that way.

But they just don't understand.

The way to come together is to push people away.

Doesn't make sense, but we've no other plan.

Hey, where you goin'?

Come back, coward.

Don't leave us alone.

There goes the key to all our power.

All our power.

All our power.

Well, damn.

Inspired by ATARI BYTES episode 187: WIZARD OF WOR, which, for all you uptight language types, is misspelled on purpose. 'cause it's cool.

SLOTTED

Lance flipped the light switch at the top of the basement stairs. The bulb in the overhead lighting at the bottom of the stairs flashed once, twice, then died. "Crud," Lance said.

"Never mind," Tim grunted and pushed past his

brother, using his phone as a flashlight. "Let's just find it and go."

"Lead on, older brother," Lance said following his sibling down the stairs. "Age before beauty."

"We're both card-carrying AARP drones, buddy," Tim said, turning the dial on the billiard-themed swag lamp over the pool table.

As light spilled over the edges of the pool table, illuminating some of the basement's game room, the men got a better look at the wood-grain paneling and brightly colored carpet depicting checkers, roulette, tic-tac-toe and poker, in repeating swatches across much of the twenty by fifteen foot room.

"Jesus," Tim said, "Dad hasn't redone this room since 1975."

"Well, in a way he did," Lance countered. He held up an original Thighmaster. "How long do you think he's had this?"

"Fat bastard," Tim said. "How'd he even muster the energy to carry that down here?"

The room was littered with cardboard boxes, a treadmill, racks of their late mother's old clothing – why Dad never got rid of it, they'd never know – and various other odds and ends.

"It's not here," Lance said.

"'course not," Tim said. "This is the crap he piled down here the last few years. The older stuff is in the back room."

Lance scratched at his stubble. "Yeah….and I think I know where." He shoved aside a punching bag with Mr. T's likeness on it and stepped through swinging saloon doors to the other half of the basement. Tim gave Mr. T a left jab and chuckled to himself as T bounced into the Garfield switch plate on the wall.

In the storage room, Tim tripped over a croquet set. Who keeps a croquet set in the basement?

Lance guffawed. It wasn't pretty.

"Keep laughing, little brother," Tim said, "And I'll turn your butt into a croquet mallet holder."

Composing himself, Lance dug a tissue from his jeans pocket, blew his nose and shoved it back in.

Tim glanced at his phone. "We better step on it," he said.

"Yeah, yeah," Lance said. "I think it's right over…" Something caught his eye. "Hey, is that Toss Across?" referring to the bean bag tic-tac-toe game. "We're getting close."

"You and that stupid toss across," Tim said. "Wussy game."

"Dad loved it," Lance said, a little defensively.

"He tolerated it 'cause you liked it," Tim corrected. "Played it for hours just to make you happy."

"He did stuff with you too," Lance said.

Tim snorted at that.

Lance bent down with a middle-aged grunt and picked up a box; the fondue pot and accessories within clattered. "You want this?"

"That was Mom's thing, not mine," Tim said. He looked at his watch again. "Seriously, we need to get moving."

"I'm going, I'm going," Lance said, opening plywood doors on the storage unit their father built when Lance and Tim were kids, during one of his longer, "I'll just be in the basement a few minutes" sessions. "Oh. My. God," Lance said and reached two trembling hands toward a box.

There it was. The 1/32 scale Atlas 1965m 1200 series slot car race set. Fully assembled, it easily took up a 10 X 10 section of the rec room. Of course, it hadn't been fully assembled since about 1978 when, in a fit of pique, Tim stomped on a curved section of track and broke it. Tim was kind of a jerk. Now and forever. Their dad was so mad when that happened. After the yelling – and Tim's incessant laughing – Dad built an armoire.

"It's all here," Lance whispered, sliding the lid off the faded cardboard box.

The photo on the lid promised hours of entertainment. And it didn't lie. Looking back, it seemed like he and Dad spent literally days setting up the track and accessories: the grandstand, the little refreshment stand, even the miniature restrooms. Dad's favorite car was the Dodge Coronet in cream. Lance always liked the Corvette Stingray with the green stripe. Dad and Lance laughed and talked and kidded each other about the races.

Then that day came when Tim broke the track. "Why can't we just get another piece?" Lance asked. But Dad just moped and shoved the remaining pieces back in the box. "I got my allowance…" Lance offered to no avail. They never played with the track again.

Dad spent an increasing amount of time in the basement alone after that. Tim didn't seem to care. Lance tried not to. Their mom…well, she was just Mom. Same as always.

Until she died.

"Even the little bottles of car oil are here," Lance said, almost squealing.

"Can we go now please?" Tim said. "I think I heard something."

"Yeah, let me just put this in my trunk."

"Yeah, I don't think so," Tim said.

"Huh?" Lance was confused.

"The track. It's going with me."

"Why do you want it?"

"Dad gave it to me," Tim said. "A couple years ago, I showed him on E-bay where he could get a new section of shoulder track to replace the broke part."

"That you broke."

"That got broke," Tim corrected. "So he said, 'sure go ahead and take it. I haven't touched that thing in decades.'"

"But it's still down here," Lance pointed out.

"So?" Tim said.

"So, you must not want it that bad. Let me take it."

"No," Tim said, picking up the box. "Dad meant it for me."

"You never cared about this track before."

"Doesn't matter."

"I want it," Lance said.

"Come get it, doofus," Tim said.

"Seriously?" Lance said.

Tim laughed. "Let's get out of here." He started to walk toward the swinging doors that lead to the rec room.

Lance shot out with an open hand and slapped Tim on the shoulder.

"Back off, little brother," Tim said.

"I said, I want that track," Lance said. He shoved his brother down. The Atlas box balancing on his other arm fell to the floor, the shells for a red and a blue car and some of the track pieces slid through a ripped corner of the box.

"Still a whiny klutz," Tim said, laughing that laugh; the older brother laugh that drove Lance insane. "Pick it up."

"I'll pick you up," Lance muttered.

"What does that…?" Tim started to ask when Lance barreled into him, shoving the bigger man off balance. "What the f - " he grunted as he fell to the floor, smacking his head on the concrete. Tim was still.

"Hey, man, you okay?" Lance said, standing over his brother.

Tim groaned, then shot out an arm, grabbing Lance's leg, sending him to the floor as well. The fifty-somethings, fifty-something-fought on the floor for a couple minutes. Then, sweaty and winded, Tim finally said. "Wait. Wait. Knock it off. We don't have time for this."

Lance panted and calmed himself. "You're right. Sorry."

Tim looked at his brother. "You know. You're right. The track should go with you. It always meant more to you than me."

"Thanks, man," Lance said.

"Whatever. Let's just get out of here."

Then men marched upstairs, stepping over the body of their dead father. "Thanks, Dad," Lance said, clutching the slot car box.

"The new finish on the cabinets looks great," Tim said, walking through the kitchen to the front door. "Too bad you can't finish them."

"That's on you," Lance said. "You always mess things up. I just came here for the track."

Tim shrugged. "What can I say? I'm chaotic good."

"That's debatable."

The sound of police sirens drifted into the house from a distance.

As Tim pulled open the front door, the sirens burst in, now coming from the driveway. "You had to find that stupid track," he muttered.

"Huh. That reminds me, I didn't see the police car slot down there," Lance said. "Dammit."

Despite the broken section, the track eventually brought a decent price on E-Bay.

Inspired by ATARI BYTES episode 188: SLOT RACERS

DISPENSE WITH THIS

The sun baked the Egyptian desert – hot even for the peak of summer in this part of the world. Babu and Adom, as if daring the sun god Ra to sweat the life out of them a bit faster, stood atop a sandy bluff overlooking, well, more sand in the Valley of Kings below. The eyes of both men were locked on the ancient ushubati statue, a servant to the dead in the afterlife, perched on the cliff's edge.

"You ever watch *Looney Tunes*?" Adom asked his brother, knowing full well Babu had, having grown up together in Syracuse.

"What?" Babu said, either through genuine confusion or unwillingness to engage.

"*Looney Tunes,*" Adom said. "You know, cartoons. Bugs Bunny. Daffy Duck. Yosemite Sam. Those guys."

"I guess," Babu said.

"Well, remember the one where Yosemite's all like, 'I'ma gonna rob that train.' And Bugs goes 'And I'm going to save that train.'? You and me, we're kind of like that."

Babu shook his head, smiled a little. "I'm walking out of here with that statue," he said. "You know that."

Adom stuck his hands in his pockets and squinted into the sunlight for a moment before answering. "Well, that's pretty much what Yosemite said. And you know how things always worked out for him."

Growing up, Adom wanted to be an archaeologist. Okay, truth: he wanted to be Indiana Jones. Who didn't? He also liked the short-run series of movies on network TV with Louis Gossett Jr. as adventuring anthropologist Gideon Oliver. Whatever the inspiration, Adom couldn't wait to go to college.

Babu was a different story.

"Why can't you be more like Adom?" their mother often asked after teen-aged Babu's latest arrest. Babu finished high school, but spent the following summer racking up petty criminal charges: vandalism, trespassing, shoplifting key lime pie flavored yogurt and Elmer Fund-shaped Pez dispensers. Typical stuff like that.

"Adom walks with the aid of the gods,' Babu once told his mom back then. "It's right there in the name. Me? I am but a child." He laughed.

His mother smirked and got up to leave the room before she said something she'd regret.

"Hey," Babu called. "Do we have any yogurt?"

When Adom finished his undergraduate studies, he invited Babu to a gathering of his friends at a cabin upstate.

"Why'd you invite me up here?" Babu asked as the sun set.

"You're my brother," Adom said. "Thought you might want to share my graduation with me."

"I don't really fit in with your college buddies, do I?"

"Well, they did like the omelets."

It was true. Babu made killer veggie omelets.

"You know what I mean."

"Man, the only one hung up on your record is you."

The encroaching darkness obscured Babu's smirk and hushed any further conversation. Just being there together was enough.

The next few years rumbled along. Adom sifted through the sands looking for artifacts and Babu floated from meaningless job to meaningless job. The years, the sands, the jobs; none left much of an impression even as life's currents pushed the brothers apart.

Adom got on the tenure track for full professorship in anthropology.

Babu went to prison for grand larceny.

"Why?" Adom asked on one of his visits to his brother – visits his brother protested every time.

"Why what?"

Adom gestured around. "What do you think?"

Babu scoffed. Then his face got quite serious. He seemed to really consider the question. "I think in my life, I missed some things: a good job, maybe college. Mom's respect…more weekends at that cabin with my brother. So I was trying to replace those things with whatever I could find. Or steal." He glanced around to see who might be listening. "Allegedly."

Adom rocked back in his chair, stunned by such naked honesty. "Whoa."

"Or, you know, maybe I just like stealing stuff."

When Babu got out of prison, Adom got him a part-time gig at the lab where the anthropology department cleans the fossils. He ran errands, cleaned the lab, made copies of syllabi for Adom's classes. Whatever.

One day, Adom asked Babu to find his passport and book him a flight to Cairo. "Some promising finds in the Valley of Kings," he said. "The team and I are leaving tonight before the other teams move in and lay claim."

"Sweet," Babu said. "Thought I might go to the new food truck on the corner. You know, before all the veggie egg rolls are gone."

"Grab me a couple," Adom said. "I'll eat 'em on the way to the airport. Hey, that plane ticket? I gotta move." Adom rushed off to find his favorite whisk broom and sifter.

"Yeah," Babu muttered. "I gotta move too."

Cut to thirty-six hours later. A cliff's edge and two brothers.

"I know a guy who'll pay big for that ushubati statue," Babu said.

"And then what?" Adom asked.

Babu was stumped for a moment. "World travel," he finally said.

Adom laughed. "Until yesterday, except for prison, you'd never been out of Syracuse."

"You got what you needed," Babu said. The job. The respect. Now I get mine."

"What is it you need, Babu?"

"Cash," Babu said, running toward the statue.

Adom sighed and stuck out one leg. Babu stumbled spectacularly, face-planting in the sand, a couple feet from the ushubatti, which wobbled a bit, but didn't fall.

Babu glared at his brother who just shrugged. "Hey," Adom said, "remember when we were kids and you got busted for stealing Pez dispensers? I thought my brother was so cool."

"You have a very strange cool-meter."

"Maybe," Adom said and reached into an interior pocket of his field vest. "I thought my brother was so cool, in fact, that I went out and ripped off my own." He pulled out of the vest pocket a Porky Pig Pez dispenser. "Been carrying this around ever since."

Babu smirked. "Mom said I should be like you, not the other way round."

"I'm still cuter," Adom said.

"The Pez in that thing has got to be gross by now."

Adom laughed. "Not really the point. Point is: you're a screw up. I'm a screw up."

Babu looked at his brother, then Porky Pig, then his brother again. "You're not going to let me have the ushubati are you?"

"Hell, no," Adom said. "But how 'bout some Pez?"

The Pez was stale, but the ushubati didn't fall.

Life was already looking up.

Inspired by ATARI BYTES episode 189: DESERT FALCON

THE FINAL MOMENT BEFORE OBLIVION OR WHATEVER ACTUALLY COMES NEXT

Staring into the face or the chasm, a void of total destruction …

What would I think about?

I guess I'd like to say I'd think about my family. But, really, I'm not sure I would.

This is not narcissism; it's practicality.

I'd like to think they'd take comfort in knowing I spent that last moment still trying to figure out how to get out of that last moment without being destroyed.

Guess that didn't work out so well, did it? Sorry.

But is that really what I'd do?

Maybe I'd wish for more moments. But is that against the rules?

Is it like how the genie says you can't wish for more wishes?

Would I spend the final moment wondering what comes after the final moment?

Seems a little late then, doesn't it?

Besides, I stopped wondering about that a long time ago. Whatever there is, it's coming whether I think about it or not.

But maybe I'd spend that final moment wondering if the end of the moment I'm in will hurt.

But do I really want to know?

Whoever is in charge of such things would probably tell me what I wanted to hear.

And that would probably be a lie, like when your parents tell you that a vaccination or blood test won't hurt.

I might spend the last moment berating an underling, even if it wasn't her fault.

I hope not, but I might.

Even at the end, some people can't accept their own failures.

Maybe I'd spend the last moment wondering what I did wrong. Or right.

Today or ever.

That'd be fun.

You know what would suck?

If I didn't know the last moment was THE LAST MOMENT.

That seems unfair, but it's far more common, I suppose.

Just going about your life then…nothing.

Life is unfair after all.

Life is an a-hole much of the time.

Would I leave a final message for the survivors like in a movie set after an alien invasion?

One of those grainy videos with the weary bearded dude surrounded by devastation,

Warning the movie's hero about the fate which befell this world?

No, I don't think I would. Here's why:

After aliens decimate Earth, Internet service would probably be awful.

What would I say? Sorry, we totally choked on the fighting the aliens thing.

I'd feel bad enough when I'm alive about the mess I'm leaving;

Let me not have to feel bad about it posthumously.

If I'm dead, I want to be remembered in a happier moment.

I think dead people deserve that. Well, most of them.

I don't mean I'd spend the final moment telling jokes or passing out candy. Or cash.

Just that I'd like to spend that final moment not degrading all the moments that came before.

Maybe nod politely. Stand and let my second in command have a seat.

Hell, maybe take a bow. At the final curtain call.

We gather all our stuff; all our friends and family.

And we know someday we'll leave it all behind.

Can't take it with you, right?

But in the end, all that other stuff goes somewhere else anyway.

And all we really leave behind is a memory.

I'd like mine to be a good one.

Inspired by ATARI BYTES episode 190: GORF. I don't think the game was this heavy. That's what I mean when I say you never quite know what kind of story I'll be inspired to write from week to week.

FAMILY TERROR…
I MEAN, FUN

MEMO FROM: Carl McMasters, advertising manager

TO: Vicki Collins, production manager

Vicki – Here's the ad copy for new client's commercial. As you know, when Leonard returned from his surprise three-day absence, he was quite keen on signing this new client even though Leonard had refused in the past. All he really said was that during his time off he'd had time to reflect on choices he'd made about this one in the past and this client persuaded him running their ads would be a beneficial move to all concerned.

Side note: I mentioned that we missed his wife's legendary potato salad at the company picnic last week. He looked very sad, but didn't explain why. She seems to have been in an accident or something..

Anyway, here's the copy. You can let me know if you'd recommend any changes, but I kind of doubt they'll get made.

Come on down to Gangster Alley, the town's premiere bowling alley. And ONLY bowling alley, now that Stan at BowlTown decided to retire and leave the state. He understood we were making an offer he couldn't refuse. Best wishes, Stan!

What's that? You don't like bowling? What's the matter with you? Bowling is so much fun, you'll die laughing. Or crying. Whatever. Basically, if the boss wants you dead, you're dead.

Twenty-five gorgeous lanes in a state-of-the-art sports facility resting atop that old gravel pit outside of town. You know the old gravel pit, right? If not, we'll be thrilled to show you around sometime.

These are some of the toughest lanes in town, slick with the sweat of our competitors. You're sure to have hours of challenging fun.

We've got concrete shoes, I mean, bowling shoes, to fit every size. Why bring your own when you can rent ours? Understood?

At Gangster Alley, our prices can't be beat. You'll pay whatever we charge. And be happy about it.

Hey, you look hungry. Yes. I said you look hungry. Why not visit our restaurant? Seriously. Do it. Burgers, nachos, homemade onion rings. You'll be proud to call our menu offerings your last meal...for today.

And we just finalized a deal with a beer distributor who owes us a favor. We'll pass the savings on to you! Hey, look at that. Now YOU owe us a favor.

Tell your bowling buddies you'll "spare" them this time if they buy the next round.

Meanwhile, the kids will love the new arcade, now featuring kiddie rides like the headless rocking horse and the merry-go-round and one we're calling the tommy gun because the fun is rapid fire!

So, come on down to Gangster Alley where you'll always bowl a strike first...before the other guy strikes you.

Inspired by ATARI BYTES episode 191: GANGSTER ALLEY

BAD POETRY CORNER:
NO MATCH FOR ME

You've got your spelling bees and sports contests.

Dance shows, choir and all the rest.

But for me, there's only one competition that truly soars.

And that, my friends, is a good game of Hunt & Score.

Doesn't matter what you call it. What's in a name?

Memory, Concentration, or even just Match Game.

In college, they called me Hunt & Score

'cause I was the best at ladies, games and more.

No one plays the game like me. My focus is fierce.

I destroy my opponents; send 'em home in a hearse.

At making card matches, I'm one-of-a-kind.

Bro, puttin' things in order is how I unwind.

Challenge me? You don't have the guts.

Make you so nervous, you'll get a thousand paper cuts.

I can match anything on a card.

Don't you know nothin's too hard.

Animals, vehicles, occupations too.

Once I even matched monkey butts and poop in a zoo.

Wherever there's a table full of overturned cards

My play is swift and intense; shatter glass into shards.

And you know, of course, I can match those bits up too.

If you oppose me, you'll be royally screwed.

My girl never understood why I do what I do.

Guess matching hearts with hers made me a fool.

Do I think it's ironic a man so alone

Makes his life about matches, not picking up a phone?

I don't know about that, but one thing's for sure…

I've paired up my soul with Hunt & Score.

Inspired by ATARI BYTES episode 192: HUNT & SCORE

BAD POETRY CORNER: OTTO RACING

In line at the grocery store
 Or commuting in an Uber car
On some other routine chore
When your mind does wander far

That feeling where you're not quite there
Mentally on the way to the next place
Not feeling happy or sad where you are
Just another rat joining in the race

Otto Racing junior the second
(His paternity is quite complicated)
Feels being in the moment is overrated
The next thing to happen beckons.

It's a feeling that exists all the time.
As a kid, Otto Racing was called Otto Racing
Out of his highchair he did climb.

In trike races beat every kid he was facing.

Skipped training wheels, went right to bikes
Couldn't sit still; didn't want to try
Always parted the trees for others on hikes
Skinned knees were no bother; no time to cry

A lead-footed driver, he was for sure.
From A to B, a straight line will do
If he could just get there, that'd be the cure
But only top speed could get you through

Legs bounce under tables.
Fingers drum up above.
Leave the room? He's not able.
As much as his brain might give him a shove.

Always smart and clever, but could never focus
The thoughts swirl like toilet water
Normal chit chat is a bunch of hocus pocus
Not cold-hearted, but people are a bother.

Otto Racing's not shy, not really, you know.

Just a bit isolated and aloof, it's fair to say.

So much to think about, places for thoughts to go.

A bit tired he is of his brain getting its way.

As a kid, Otto Racing's bike moved so fast.

His life, it did too.

No time to look at the past.

There's too much to do.

Inspired by ATARI BYTES episode 193: AUTO RACING

IT'S THE JOURNEY, NOT THE DESTINATION

The summer air was thick and humid, making the darkness a heavy blanket my friends and I fought to kick off. The bright streetlights and storefronts provided a stark contrast to the blackness around us; like if you bite into a cupcake with orange frosting and discover it's mint-flavored. I was fifteen and wild. Okay, not that wild. But that night, I thought I was unstoppable.

Stengle, Amy and I ducked for cover into the sub shop just in time. The lightning from the oncoming storm competed with the glow from the band Journey's tour bus for supremacy at blinding all of us.

"That concert was…UH-mazing!" Amy cried, drawing a scowl from the old, bearded dude putting the crucial tomato on a BLT. Running for blocks and blocks, dodging weirdo roadies, had left us drenched in sweat. Amy fanned her stomach with the tail of her Journey concert shirt. For a fleeting moment, I thought – hoped? – she might take it off. She didn't. Dammit.

"Yeah, like amazing we're not dead," Stengle said. Stengle liked to exaggerate, though tonight I wasn't sure he was far off. He folded himself in half and lowered down onto one of the restaurant chairs that suddenly looked way too small. It fit me just right, though, unfortunately.

Then we heard the roar of a huge vehicle launching skyward.

How had all this happened?

All together, my friends and I made the you're-about-to-see-a-flashback sound effect from TV. Like really loud. Tomato guy was not happy.

I don't know how – or why – my dad scored Journey tickets for us. I would probably have to mow the lawn every day for the rest of my life to make up for it, but it was worth it. Steve Perry was in fine form that night. Steve Smith kept the band in line, Jonathan Cain was on point, Ross Valory looked a little bored, but still sounded pretty good. Neal Schon only messed up once, but I don't think anyone else noticed.

After everything that happened that night, though, the concert was an after-thought.

We hung around a long time after the show was over. We knew we had time. My dad would take forever to find the Shakey's Restaurant where he was supposed to pick us up.

"Dude, I just saw Ross getting on the tour bus," Stengle said as we dodged the after-concert traffic.

"No, you didn't," Amy said.

"Yes, I did,", Stengle said. "Getting on that…bus thing. You know…" Stengle didn't really know how to finish that sentence. But I couldn't really blame him.

The "tour bus" was a colossal winged vehicle with rocket boosters. Probably not street legal for mere mortals. But c'mon. This was JOURNEY.

"We could have gotten on there," Stengle said thoughtfully.

"The bus?" I said. "No way." Amy just laughed.

"Well, yeah," Stengle said, "if it hadn't been for that three-headed roadie screaming at us."

"Sure, if it'd only been TWO heads," I said, "you could have gotten right past him I bet. Right now, you'd be playing Ross' bass." Amy and I high fived, which was glorious.

"Mock me all you want," Stengle said. "But remember, I'm the one who scaled the stage barrier."

It was true. Little surprised we didn't get thrown out right then, but Steve just sort of rolled with it. The shifty-eyed promoter that's always hanging around at these concerts, though, looked extra-shifty eyed. Until his eyes fell out of his head.

I glanced out the window of the sub shop and saw... the Kool-Aid Man? I dunno. Pretty sure that's what it was.

"Hey, kid," the tomato-slinger said. "Are you and your friends going to order something or not?"

I grinned at Amy who just shrugged. "Yeah, sure," I said. "Gimmie a double decker triple decker." I laughed. It seemed funny. Tomato guy didn't think so.

"No burgers," he said. "Just subs. You want ham, turkey or roast beef?"

The lower half of a sesame seed bun floated down from the ceiling. A sizzling beef patty followed, landing right on top of the bun. Plop. The old guy's beloved tomato came after that.

There was something familiar about all that. A game or something? I wasn't sure. "No burgers, huh?" I said. "Whaddaya call that?" The old guy ignored me.

Stengle bolted outside, running up and down the sidewalk. "It's raining," he shouted. "It's raining dollar bills, y'all!" He stuck out his tongue as if he could catch them like snowflakes.

I opened the sub shop door and yanked Stengle back in. "Ow," he said, tongue still wagging. "I bit my tongue."

"It's not raining money, dingus," I said.

"Duh," Amy said, pointing. "it's raining provolone."

She was right. Thick slices of the smoked Italian delight slapped us in the face.

Then the old tomato guy's – no, he didn't actually turn into a tomato, if you're wondering. That would be weird. The old tomato guy's sandwiches leapt off the cutting board, grew fangs and ate us.

Tomato guy laughed. Steve Perry came in, grabbled one of those thick, chocolate chip cookies by the cash register and laughed at us too. Then he flew away on a magic carpet.

Oh, yeah, we we're all pretty stoned. Did I mention that? Some dude behind at us at the concert shared a joint with us. I don't think anyone will notice.

Insert your own snippet of a Journey song here.

Inspired by ATARI BYTES episode 194: JOURNEY ESCAPE. There really is an Atari video game inspired by the band Journey. No, really. Go listen to the episode.

WINDMILL OF DEATH

Paddy was just twelve-years-old. A life of fear was the only life she'd ever known. Crouched now in the dark with her little brother and her parents, waiting for the next one to hit, she wondered how much longer that life would last.

"Hush now," Paddy's mother, Juno, whispered. "This round should be over soon." The bit of sunlight coming through the window high atop the windmill glinted off the clip in Juno's green-streaked hair. She straightened the bun atop Paddy's curly, lavender hair and Paddy wriggled, annoyed by the fussing.

Paddy's little brother Maddox groaned. "Quiet, Maddox. You'll kill us all," she said, a bit more of a tremor in her voice than she would have liked.

Her father, Colin, wore the same worried expression he always wore. He looked upward, head slightly cocked as the blades of the old windmill creaked and groaned. How many times had the family huddled here in the dark? How many more times could they survive? He combed nervously at his beard with thin, well-worked fingers.

WHAM!

The windmill shook as the projectile slammed into one of the blades. The turbine kept on spinning, though. They were all right, the four of them, this time.

Paddy's family had maintained the windmill for generations. It was a solitary existence. The windmill caretakers occasionally interacted with the knights in the castle over the hill or the elves in the Candyland castle to the south, but not often. Each of them had their part to play defending their own patch of this green expanse and they would do so, no matter how taxing.

The family held its collective breath as a chartreuse-colored sphere filled the opening in one of the lower windows, rattled there a bit, but thankfully did not enter. The angry shouts of the men outside were deafening. Paddy hated them, those men, and the others who lumbered through Paddy's homeland all the days of her life without a care for its beauty. They sought only victory at any cost.

"Make it stop, make it stop," Maddox shouted. Paddy held him a bit closer. Her little brother had never known a world without the giant beasts and their metal death rods. But she, Paddy, remembered a period when the snows came and the men went away.

Two more spheres slammed the side of the windmill. "I fear this might be the end," Colin said, though, to be fair, Colin worried about everything.

Their mother started to object when an orange globe struck the blades, rode one down and through an opening in the roof of the windmill. The whole family screamed. "Remember me," Colin shouted and leapt upon the devil's own turd. The two rolled down a ramp, into a hole and out of the windmill, where they were scooped up by one of those monsters; the beast laughing and joking the whole time.

"Nooooo," Paddy screamed, but she knew it was pointless. The life of a windmill caretaker is short and brutal. It comes with the job.

Through tears, Juno attempted to rally her remaining family. "Now, children, we must honor your father. We will continue in our duties to the windmill as we must. As we always have."

Paddy nodded silently, though she didn't necessarily agree. No, Mother, she thought. Not as we always have. Things are different now. I will avenge the horrors of the metal rod people. They will pay for what they have done. They will no longer march across our grasslands with impunity. Tread lightly, beasts. I am coming for you.

Paddy stood on wobbly knees she willed to lock. And then, as she had heard the monsters outside do so many times before, she bellowed out a chilling war cry:

"FORE!"

Outside, Rachel handed her putter to Ron. "Did you hear something?" she asked.

Ron sank his golf ball into a clown's mouth. "Nope," he said. "Put me down for …a four." He took a huge lick of cherry snow cone; easily the best thing about the miniature golf course. "Did you…did you hear something?"

Rachel shrugged. "Hey, after this, you wanna hit the arcade?"

Inspired by ATARI BYTES episode 195: MINIATURE GOLF.

TOMATO PUREE

Watkins sat quietly, listening to the pounding in his head.

Wham, wham, wham.

He felt sickly hot. The very existence of light melted his eyeballs.

"I will never drink again," he muttered, wincing at the effort and the noise.

That was a lie. Working in the Vegetable Crimes Division meant wading through a lot of horrible stuff – not even including creamed cauliflower. He had to do something to clear his brain…or drown it.

His cell phone vibrated on the desk. It made his wobbly brain shimmy. That, in turn, made his stomach lurch.

"Watkins," he said into the phone in a mumble. "Talk fast. Before I die."

What Watkins heard on the other end made his mostly eighty proof blood run cold. Sobriety marched through his extremities with cleats.

"I'll be right there."

The Mobile Vegetable Crime Unit rolled to a stop at the south end of Farmer Brown's property. Watkins was barely out of the truck when a shadow washed over him.

"Watkins," Tillman boomed down from over him. "What are you doing here? There's no veggie crime here. You're out of your jurisdiction." His breath smelled of onions. The sicko. Watkins investigated vegetable related crimes; talking to Tillman was like being a cop in the vice division talking to another cop while looking at his porn collection.

"Back off, Tillman. I can help."

Tillman chuckled. It was the hollow laugh of a man who long ago realized there is nothing really funny in this world, but the façade of humor sometimes is the only thing standing between getting through each day and going completely insane.

Tillman turned and waved a beefy arm in a sweeping gesture toward the acreage before them. "Really, Watkins? Be my guest. These tomatoes have been pureed."

Watkins' intestines puckered. Row after row of tomato plants were decimated. Ripe, red beefsteak tomatoes reduced to the red sludge of a cheap horror show. It was worse than he'd expected.

Watkins barfed. A lot. Loud, wet, dry heaves floated on rivers of bile. When he was finished, he wiped his chin with a wrinkled, discount store suit coat sleeve.

"Like I said," Tillman said, "Get out of here. Tomatoes are fruit, not veggies. You know that. Besides..." He made a face. "Clearly, you're not up for it."

Watkins stood on wobbling knees. "No," he said. "This time...it's personal."

*****

Back at the station, Watkins swiped through the photos on his phone. The car he bought after he made lieutenant. Sea shells from the trip to the ocean. Poops that look like dolphins.

As he scrolled, his thumb hovered over his favorite photo. In this one, he saw his girlfriend Gina and two of the firmest, roundest, most gorgeous tomatoes he'd ever seen....they were beefsteak, fresh picked.

The photo was from that day Watkins, Gina and the newly harvested tomatoes spent the day at the beach; the humans frolicking in the surf, the tomatoes ripening in the sun. The capper for the day was a visit to the comedy club where they heckled that hack prop comic. The tomatoes especially loved that.

Tomatoes originated in Peru, so Watkins, Gina and the tomatoes enjoyed a Peruvian meal. The lomo saltado was excellent.

But then the solterito, a Peruvian salad, showed up.

And their salad got tossed.

Maybe the tomatoes were too ripe. Maybe the chilis were too spicy or the cheese not spicy enough. Maybe it was because the chef was Swedish and unaccustomed to South American cuisine. He was certainly flustered and speaking incoherently.

Whatever it was, that salad tossed the room like… something Peruvian that tosses other things. Beans and cheese smeared the walls as the salad pinwheeled across the room. The tomatoes were sliced and diced.

And Gina…well, it turned out Gina was allergic to fava beans.

The chef - who just happened to be Swedish and had absolutely no connection to any beloved characters from popular culture who are both Swedish and chefs, living or dead, real or fiction – stood off to the side, laughing.

The chef from Sweden fled back to, well, Sweden apparently. Watkins gave chase, but lost him. And that wasn't all he lost.

Gina and the two tomatoes. All three were gone.

Every day. Every single day. Watkins told himself he could have, should have, done something different. Should have known what was going to happen. Should have protected Gina and the 'maters. He knew who was behind the attack. Knew it as well as he knew the difference between tomato paste and tomato puree.

Gina wouldn't have liked him being consumed by thoughts of revenge. The tomatoes, well, they wouldn't care; they were tomatoes. The highly acidic nature of tomatoes may cause the fruit to repeat on you, but Watkins couldn't repeat that day.

Watkins could, however, avenge those slaughtered heirlooms in that field turned graveyard.

"They'll never even be tomato sauce," he muttered. "And no baby ketchup packets. This isn't right."

And Watkins knew just what to do.

The Wriggling Nest was a hotspot in a cold, hostile part of town. Not a bright spot, mind you. The tomato-seedy nightclub hosted thousands of young people and twice as many worms every single week. But if you weren't part of the "in" crowd – as evidenced by using the term "in" to signify acceptance – you stood out like a golden yellow slicer tomato in a garden full of green tomatoes.

Watkins was definitely not one of the "in" crowd.

"Where's Weston?" Watkins asked the fat corn earworm working the door at the Wriggling Nest. Weston was the club's owner and a known crime boss. But much like cauliflower, Watkins had never been able to touch him. Also, both turned his stomach.

"Weston who?" the earworm coyly responded.

Watkins shot out an arm, fingers gripping where a neck might be if worms had necks. "Don't mess with me. I been lookin' for a drain tube for my garbage disposal. You might just fit the bill."

"Let him in, Sebastian," a voice said from inside the empty club. The patrons wouldn't start showing up for hours. Weston was always there, seemed never to sleep. He was a fruitworm perpetually in the larvae stage, seeming never to age, yet with eyes that had seen it all, and deemed most of it beneath contempt. Fruit worms might have five hearts, but all of Weston's were black as the topsoil tomatoes thrive in.

Watkins stepped past Sebastian into the club. The subdued daytime lighting was unsettling. Weston slithered from behind the bar. "You're here about the heirlooms, aren't you?"

"They were slaughtered last night."

"Yes, and I know how your heart bleeds red as marina," Weston said.

"They were innocent," Watkins said through gritted teeth. "Whatever the beef is with you and the beefsteaks, the heirlooms didn't deserve this."

"Plump thing with a navel," Weston said. "That's what the Aztec name for 'tomato' translates as. Fitting for such a useless fruit."

Watkins swung one leg out, sweeping Weston to the floor and stepping on the worm's midsection. "If I want to learn a language, I'll get Rosetta Stone. From you, I just want answers. Who carried out the hit?"

Weston laughed. "You know already."

"Tell me."

"It wasn't me," Weston said innocently. "Sometimes, though, family can be our greatest ally, but also our greatest enemy."

"You're saying the beefsteaks did this?"

"I'm not saying anything. We're just talking. May I get up now?"

Watkins lifted his boot off Weston's slimy clitellum with a wet, sucking sound. Weston rose back to his… feet? Balancing on one end anyway.

"Cops like you," Weston said. "You think you know the criminals on sight. That they're easy to spot, like the deviled eggs in a garden salad. But sometimes, you're so distracted by the eggs, you miss the salmonella on the tomatoes."

The cherry tomatoes on the roof of Watkins car roared through the night. Why it was already night when he had just left the Wriggling Nest in the daytime is one of those story things you don't need to worry about.

As he flew around corners, grinding up miles, conflicting feeling ground up his soul. Why would the beefsteaks do this? His little tomatoes, the innocent little fruits gathering sand on that beach, they would never have done this.

But did he really know that? They were tomatoes. It's not like he could have asked them, "Hey, are you tomatoes cold-blooded murderers?" Life is hard. Befriending tomatoes even harder.

Watkins rolled to a stop at the edge of the beefsteak plantation. He pulled his service weapon and stepped briskly from the vehicle. Police or not, he was going to avenge the heirlooms. Whatever slight the beefsteaks thought the heirlooms had committed, they didn't deserve the punishment the beefsteaks meted out.

A little voice in Watkins's head noted he was about to slaughter beefsteak tomatoes for doing the same thing to heirlooms. He locked that little voice in a closet in his brain; the same closet where he kept sex dreams about furniture.

Watkins stepped over an irrigation ditch, gun at the ready. But the cry of anguish that poured forth fertilized the dark patches of his soul. No doubt more cynicism and hopelessness would grow in those areas forever more when he thought about what he saw there this day.

"Damn you," Watkins groaned. "Damn you all to hell."

The beefsteak tomatoes were gone. The whole crop

self-harvested. The tomatoes took their revenge and split. And not the good kind of split, like to go on a turkey sandwich. They rolled on to the next town to poison more people – and not just by confusing them with the whole "is it a fruit or a vegetable?" thing.

But they will return one day to wreak havoc. And when they do, Watkins will be waiting with a can of vinaigrette to rain down on them like Hell's own juices.

That's a promise.

Inspired by ATARI BYTES episode 196: REVENGE OF THE BEEFSTEAK TOMATOES

WHO WILL BE TANK'S PLUS ONE?

The image that came up on the computer screen was a beach at sunset, nothing around but tread marks in the sand leading off into the distance. Seemed harmless enough, she thought. With a deep breath, she started entering information:

Turn Ons: Master Power Toggle Switch

Turn Offs: Heavy cannons. Anyone who is mean to animals.

My Favorite Thing to Do Is: Carrying the soldiers who lead the fight to liberate the masses and bring democracy to the world

Least Favorite Thing to Do: Laundry

What I want from a Relationship: Cessation of hostilities

My ideal date: Rolling across the desert at dusk. You and me shooting our loads in the night.

My Ideal Plus One: My ideal plus one is strong, fearless, ready to charge into any situation and come out on top, no matter the terrain. He should also like sushi.

Tank completed her dating profile and registered her account so she could read the responses. If there were any. For her profile pic, she uploaded a snapshot of herself atop Hill 42 looking, she hoped, brave and powerful. And, honestly, sexy.

Tank navigated away from "TankPlusOne.com" and closed her laptop, obliterating it with her high-caliber, turret mounted gun. "Oops. Dammit." That was the third computer this week.

Tank hated dating profiles. She never knew what to say. Why bother? Did anyone really want to date a tank? Sure, her name was "Tank" and she was a tank. People knew that when they saw her. And most of the time that was okay. But sometimes…sometimes maybe she could be a howitzer. Or one of those Civil War cannons. They were so cool.

Not that Tank didn't like who she was. Not that she wanted to be anyone else. She commanded respect, sure. Her defenses against anti-tank ammo were strong. But others were also a little…afraid…of her. Tank didn't always like that. She just…wondered what it would be like to be someone else. You know? No harm in that, is there?

Tank launched a lightweight shell straight up, then waited for Trevor to text back. Soon, the explosive answer came: "S'up," Trevor said.

"Well, I did it," Tank said.

"The dating app?"

"Yes. The dating app," Tank said. "Did I make a mistake?"

"Levelling the Burger Hut on Route 9 was a mistake."

"Well, it does look a lot like an enemy headquarters… except for the plastic burger wearing a hat," Tank said in her own defense.

"Anyway…the dating app thing is not a mistake," Trevor said. "It could be good for you."

"Do you think so?"

"I know so," Trevor said.

"You also said you knew you'd marry a vintage Cadillac."

"I'm still holding out for that one," Trevor said. "What's the worst that could happen?"

"Complete humiliation," Tank said. "melting myself into scrap metal in disgust."

"Well, sure, but even if the date is awful, you might get some free diesel out of it."

"This is dumb," Tank said. "I should just delete that stupid profile. I'm busy anyway. Got a lot of stuff to blow up."

And then Tank's phone chimed – a response from TankPlusOne.com. Someone actually responded to her profile.

Boom.

Inspired by ATARI BYTES episode 197: TANK PLUS because everyone deserves someone.

LEAVE IT ALL ON THE FIELD

Nick stroked his beard and brushed the end of it off the drawing table, cocking his head as he sized up the cartoon in progress. As the town paper's newest editorial cartoonist, he had the extra pressure of not just bringing the funny, but also bringing THE MOMENT, that point in the cartoon when the humor crescendoed to a punchline that really meant something. He wasn't there yet with this one.

Maybe coffee would help.

Nick rose and stretched, wincing at a twinge in his back – thanks old, college soccer injury – and went to find a cup of coffee and maybe a flavored creamer. He hoped he'd get this cartoon done before he had to pick up Jayne from softball at four and get Ryan to little league at 4:30. Then taekwondo for all at six.

On the drawing board, a sparely drawn woman – almost ghostly – wore soccer attire and a sad expression in one corner of the page. A question mark floated in a thought balloon over her head. In another corner, a grumpy, square-jawed man in a football helmet. A third corner had a baseball player with massive, Popeye arms. The fourth corner showed bleachers full of angry-looking sports fans. And in the center of the page was a beaming cartoon caricature of a rich guy – complete with top hat and a money bag in each fist. The rich guy wore a sign that said, "Organized Sports".

Nick called the soccer player "Hedy" after legend of the silver screen Hedy Lamarr, who, in addition to being an acclaimed actress, co-invented during World War II, technology that would protect the Navy's radio-controlled torpedoes from frequency jamming attempts. (It's true. Look it up.) This had nothing to do with sports, but Nick had always had a thing for Hedy Lamarr. And she did develop a ski resort in Aspen, CO with one of her husbands (also true), so there's that.

In the comic, Hedy said, "In a normal soccer game, I head the ball eight times. I know science says that's bad for women's brains, but I can't remember why."

The baseball player with the massive arms, ironically seemed unable to lift them and pitch the ball.

In the bleachers, the crowd was a mix of people cheering, other people throwing punches, and a few waving pennants that said things like, "Money in Sports" and "Yay Player Exploitation".

The football player just grimaced, clutching his head. "Is he gone," the quarterback groaned.

"I think so," Hedy said, push kicking a soccer ball to the baseball player who just let it bounce off his chest because he couldn't lift his massive arms to catch it.

"So, seriously, what are we gonna do?" the football

player said. "I feel nauseous. Does anyone else feel nauseous?"

"We're doing it. This comic revels in the negative downside of sports while ignoring the fact that sports unites all humanity, not to mention encouraging sportsmanship and clean living," the baseball player shouted aggressively. "Has anyone seen my testicles? They're really tiny."

"No, I meant, what are we gonna do about my head? It really hurts," the football player said. "The six of us should be able to come up with something."

The baseball player and Hedy exchanged glances, but didn't say anything.

The rich guy in the middle of the cartoon pulled a pocket watch from his waistcoat, noted the time and tapped his foot. "I do believe it's game time," he said.

Hedy, the football player and the baseball player all shrugged. "What are we gonna do?" Hedy said. Then, "uh…." But she didn't know who to finish the sentence.

"We're gonna leave it all on the field," the baseball

player said. "No refunds."

The players melted back into place; frozen mid-goal, mid-touchdown, mid strike-out. On the punishing, treacherous fields of play that were the worst places for them to be and the only places they wanted to be.

Nick returned to the drawing board, wiping hazelnut spread residue on his pants. He sat in the chair with the familiar, comforting squeak and stared at his drawing. How was he going to finish?

Oh.

In bold strokes across the top of the comic panel, Nick wrote, "Leave it all on the field. No refunds."

Then he went to take his kids to sports practice.

Inspired by ATARI BYTES episode 198: PELE'S SOCCER

TRANSCRIPT OF WITNESS TESTIMONY, THE PEOPLE v. BARNABY BUILDER

Bailey Nomerci, PROSECUTOR: Please state your name.

CARL CONTRAPTION: Carl Contraption.

Court Reporter: Was that 'Carl Contraception'?

CONTRAPTION: No 'Contraption'. C-O-N-T-R-A-P-T-I-O-N. But I'm a big believer in the other.

JUDGE: The jury will disregard the witness's wink at the court reporter. Proceed, Ms. Nomerci.

NOMERCI: Mr. Contraption, do you own your own business in town?

CONTRAPTION: I do, "Neighborhood Contraption Service & Supply". Been there about seventeen years. Sell you anything you need to build anything you want.

NOMERCI: Well, we're interested today in one specific

build. Are you familiar with Barnaby Builder?

CONTRAPTION: Sure. Regular customer.

NOMERCI: Is he in the courtroom today?

Contraption points.

NOMERCI: Let the record show the witness has pointed to the defendant, Barnaby Builder. Mr. Contraption, on the afternoon of August the 4th, did you sell Mr. Builder the parts to an "Ogre Outrager" brand contraption?

CONTRAPTION: Sure did. One of our best sellers.

NOMERCI: What does the Ogre Outrager do?

CONTRAPTION: Well, when the parts of the contraption are assembled in the correct sequence, a green power button appears and allows the user to fire bullets at a target.

NOMERCI: What sort of targets?

CONTRAPTION: Could be anything.

NOMERCI: Humans?

CONTRAPTION: That's not what our products are intended for.

NOMERCI: Ogres?

CONTRAPTION: Again, not what the Outrager is for.

NOMERCI: But "Ogre" is right there in the name. It's printed here on the box.

CONTRAPTION: Poetic license. The 'ogre' on the box is clearly a cartoon.

NOMERCI: Can anyone purchase the device?

CONTRAPTION: We don't turn anyone away.

NOMERCI: And can anyone assemble the device.

CONTRAPTON: If they have the blueprint, sure.

NOMERCI: Did Mr. Builder have the blueprint?

CONTRAPTION: Yep. It's bundled with the contraption.

NOMERCI: Is the Ogre Outrager a lethal device?

CONTRAPTION: Well, it's for shooting targets.

NOMERCI: But if those targets were, say, ogres, using the contraption would kill them, wouldn't it?

CONTRAPTION: But that's not what I sell contraptions for. They're fun!

NOMERCI: Sir, there's an exploding ogre on the box…

CONTRAPTION: A CARTOON ogre…

NOMERCI: Why did you sell Mr. Builder this contraption?

CONTRAPTION: He was a paying customer.

NOMERCI: Did he tell you why he wanted it?

CONTRAPTION: I didn't ask.

NOMERCI: An ogre had been seen in the vicinity of your shop's neighborhood, hasn't it? Scaring people. Slashing tires. Using all the paper towels in the convenience store bathrooms and eating all the beef jerky.

CONTRAPTION: I heard somethin' about that yeah.

Nomerci holds up Exhibit 2.

NOMERCI: Do you recognize this t-shirt?

CONTRAPTION: Maybe…

NOMERCI: This is the t-shirt Mr. Builder was wearing the day of August 4 when he purchased the Ogre Outrager at your store, assembled and activated it. Would you read the writing on this shirt and describe the picture on it please?

CONTRAPTION: Send All the Ogres Into Orbit. There's an ogre sitting on a rocket and blasting into space.

NOMERCI: What do you think that means?

CONTRAPTION: Um, encourage more ogres to apply to the space program?

NOMERCI: I think it means Mr. Builder had it out for ogres.

CONTRAPTION: I don't know that that's true.

BUILDER: No, it totally is.

JUDGE: The defendant will refrain from interrupting.

NOMERCI: And, Mr. Contraption, despite the defendant's animus toward ogres, you sold him that contraption.

CONTRAPTION: I didn't ask what he was gonna do with it. And he never said…

BUILDER: No, I totally said I was gonna obliterate some ogres.

JUDGE: I'm warning you, Mr. Builder…

CONTRAPTION: Well, he didn't say it was THIS ogre.

BUILDER: But I showed you my membership card from the Order of Ogre Ostracizers Organization. And a photo on my phone of that one ogre knocking lattes out of people's hands.

LESLIE GETIMOFF, defense attorney: Your honor, I give up.

JURY FOREMAN: Can we just find him guilty right now?

JUDGE: Looks like we'll be out of here by lunch.

BUILDER: Can I get an ogre omelet?

LESLIE GETIMOFF: Stop talking.

Inspired by ATARI BYTES episode 199: BLUEPRINT.

A PLACE FOR EVERYTHING AND EVERYTHING IN ITS PLACE

Cheswick thought about John Lennon, as he did about many of his dead friends, after their lunches. "Imagine" instantly played through his earphones, drowning out the squeak of the wheels on his cart. The squeak pulsed in time to the objections of his arthritic knees, so the change was welcome.

As he proceeded, Cheswick quickly realized that was the wrong choice. "Imagine" wasn't doing it for him today. "Purple Rain" started to play. Not feel good pop, to be sure, but at least a little more... hopeful? And come on...Prince! Good dude, even if he never picks up a check.

Cheswick shook his head again. The music stopped and he removed the headphones. He brought his cart to a stop at the corner of the North America, present day, letter "M" section of the archive. Time to get to work.

"Right," Cheswick said. "What sort of arbitrary nonsense have they got for me today?"

The cart looked a little like an old-timey ice cream cart you might see at the county fair. In 1957.

Cheswick opened the hatch atop the cart and a bit of frosty chill wafted out. Cheswick waved it away impatiently. He reached in and pulled out a vial that looked a bit like a chartreuse glow stick with a USB thumb drive suspended within. "Hello, Ms. Violet McInerney," he said to it. "White. American. Republican. Likes raspberry iced tea and…" He cocked his head as the next attribute gave him pause. "Also likes spankings. All right then."

The wall of the "M" section slid away, like a monolith receding into the mists of time. Row upon row of glow sticks of all colors – including a few no human could perceive – stretched from floor to ceiling, not that anyone could see the ceiling from the floor. The rows were pockmarked with slots waiting for glow sticks to be inserted.

On the third row up from the floor, Cheswick found the slot designated for Ms. McInerney and inserted the stick. With a quick slurping sound, the liquid within was…well, Cheswick didn't know quite what happened to it. It seemed the wall ingested it somehow. The wall slid closed and Violet's essence became just one of the anonymous mass of humanity.

The next glow stick Cheswick retrieved was for a Pakistani man named "Arav Bukhari". Cheswick moved the cart to the appropriate section. Cheswick perceived that Arav appreciated cricket, the works of a number of Pakistani authors, and Rocky Road ice cream. Arav's glowstick went into a slot well above Cheswick's head, making his extendable arms quite handy. Literally.

Next was a Canadian named Bob – no last name, just "Bob", for reasons known only to him. Bob was a professional magician on a very local basis. He studied all kinds of magic, was very much into body piercings and the music of Coldplay. In mere moments, his glow stick's fluid disappeared – abracadabra – into the wall.

Linda Gleason likes French Impressionist painters. Pedro Gonzales is a political activist. Bart Westin wonders why his penis does that one weird thing it does.

So many different people with so many different attributes. Yet all looked the same, encased in their tubes and lined up here in their individual slots on the wall.

"Is that it?" Cheswick wondered aloud as break time rolled around and his cart was ready to be refilled. "I slot the lot. The lot I slot. And all the slotted lots I got." He shrugged. "Break time, I guess."

George Carlin brought brownies today. Cheswick hurried to get some before they were gone.

The next day on the job was the same. Bonneville rides a unicycle and leans libertarian. Slotted. Kamila is into cake decorating. Slotted. Gregor can't stand brussels sprouts and has a weird fascination with mayonnaise-based porn. Slotted.

All the glowstick-USB drive things lined up there. A slot for everyone and everyone in a slot. All these people, either alive or dead, tall or short, brown, white or whatever. They all looked the same now. Cheswick couldn't tell one from another.

And that was kind of sad.

Cheswick reached for a random glow stick. When he pulled it out, separated it from the group, the stick pulsed with…life and vitality. All the attributes that made that boring old stick a person flowed forth. And it was…beautiful.

Then he pulled out a few more. The fluid within the sticks burbled – happily it seemed to Cheswick, but he knew that sounded weird. The color was sharper though.

So, for the rest of the day, Cheswick held back a few of the glow sticks, pushed them around with him on his cart. He just liked having them around, having other people around.

But then the end of his work shift came. It was time to put the people back in their slots. Jennifer the juggler. Serge was a vegan. Chen was a flat earther and environmental activist. They would go into their slots and none of that would matter.

But something weird had happened as he pushed his cart around that day.

Cheswick came to perceive that, not only was Jennifer a good juggler, but she also liked flamenco dancing. Serge loved the *Peanuts* comic strip. Chen always wanted to be an astronaut.

Cheswick wouldn't have known any of that about these people if he just put them in their slots and forgot about them. It made him weirdly happy – like, getting a free dessert because the restaurant messes up your order happy – to have them around.

So, at the end of his shift, he took them home.

He lined the glowsticks up on the small kitchen table for one and looked at the sticks for a while. They seemed to enjoy the time out; not literally, of course, because they were just the essences of people suspended in a fluid made through a proprietary process Cheswick couldn't begin to understand. So, a little time away from the library couldn't hurt. The slots would be there for them the next day. Besides, Serge had a killer fajita recipe.

But dutifully, if reluctantly, the next morning, Cheswick said goodbye to his new friends and slotted them, all their individuality fading away.

Cheswick had just started looking for the slot for Anton Alvarez, who had issues with his mother, could fart the alphabet and was a senior congressional aide when the call came in.

Cheswick was being summoned upstairs.

That's probably not good. Well, it could be because his six-month probation was over and it was time for a raise. But probably not.

Cheswick left his cart and shuffled to the supervisor's office. "Is Marsha here?" Cheswick asked after clearing his voice, speaking in a muted mumble.

Dan looked up from his phone and smirked. "Oh, it wasn't Marsha that called you," he said. "It was...*higher up*."

Shit.

This was serious.

Cheswick didn't know who exactly was above Marsha, but he knew he didn't want to meet that person...or thing.

Still staring at his phone, Dan gestured absently to the set of double doors at the far end of the reception area. Cheswick's innards convulsed. Could have been the fajitas from last night, but probably wasn't.

Cheswick didn't quite grasp that his legs were moving, though they were. The doors swung open as he approached. Stepping through them was like stepping into outer space with nothing to ground him.

The room was either cavernous or tiny. It was hard to tell. All was black, but not dark. Cheswick's eyes adjusted, but he wasn't sure to what. He also wasn't sure how far in to walk, so he just stopped when the doors swung closed behind him.

A long pause when nothing happens. Finally, Cheswick cleared his throat.

Another pause.

Finally, a voice said, "Do you know what we do at this organization?"

The voice might have been male, maybe female. It filled the room, coming from anywhere and everywhere.

"Um," Cheswick started, unsure where to go next.

"Exactly," the voice said. "We deliver humanity."

"Right," Cheswick. "Wait. What?"

"We deliver humanity to itself," the voice said, seemingly not aware it was speaking gibberish. Maybe the voice was drunk?

The voice continued, "The humans, they are complex, but confused creatures. We provide organization and the security of knowing who they are."

"Don't they know who they are?" Cheswick really didn't understand.

"Not until we tell them," said the voice. "We preserve individuality and give it back to the populace. And you are the key. You are vital to this whole process."

It flashed through Cheswick's mind to ask whether he could get a raise to something above minimum wage if he was so damn important. The flash, though, was drowned in fear sweat.

"Why did you take the vials home?"

"Uh…"

"Yes, I know. I know everything that happens here. Why did you do it?"

"They felt lonely," Cheswick blurted.

"No. That wasn't in their character trait lists. We decide who they are."

"I think…I think those people were…more than what was in their lists."

"Not possible," the voice said.

"You're wrong."

Cheswick once got fired from a job detailing the boats that travel the River Styx because he told the manager he was a racist for supporting a demon in an upcoming election. This experience today was starting to feel like that. Well, at least he stood up for something. He could always find another job, right?

A week later, Irene slipped on a pair of work gloves because the chill from the pseudo ice cream cart made her fingers numb. She looked at the inventory and lifted out the one vial she had been given – a rush job, they said. "Skip your break," they said. "You'll get comp time," they said. "Don't worry about it."

The wall slid away and an empty slot waited. Irene looked at the vial and nodded. "Cheswick. Troublemaker. Elitist. Thinks he knows better than everyone else." Irene smirked. Well, it takes all kinds, doesn't it? "What a jerk." She inserted the vial into the wall slot. The wall did its thing.

And she never thought about Cheswick again.

Inspired by ATARI BYTES episode 201: SLOTS in the sense that the road to this story started with the word "slots" and veered widely into the weird wilderness where I spend a lot of time.

RECLUSE REFORMATION

On one knee, Magnolia Bouchard balanced a slice of pizza – sauerkraut. Seriously, the gas station had sauerkraut pizza. How cool is that? A twenty-ounce cola on the other knee leaned precariously against the steering wheel. She debated where to put the chocolate bar and chips occupying her hands at the moment.

Then her phone rang.

"Dammit," she muttered, tossing the chips to the passenger seat along with the chocolate bar. Probably cracked now, she thought bitterly. Like being the first to break the surface in a new jar of peanut butter, unwrapping a fully intact chocolate bar is a magical moment.

Magnolia answered the call. It was Becky from the office.

"Got a new call for you, Mags," Becky said. "Guy on 14th Avenue says he's got big time spider problems."

"Spiders," Mags groaned. "Why did it have to be spiders?"

"Don't discriminate," Becky said. "An extermination is an extermination."

"Not true," Mags countered. "The techniques for fighting spider infestations are markedly different than, say, wasps or terminates. "I remember one time…"

Becky cut her off. "I'm texting you the name and address. Hurry up. He sounds upset."

Mags consumed half the slice of pizza in one bite and the truck rumbled toward the address as she gulped down the rest. The life of an exterminator is like that:

making things disappear, be they food or pests… sometimes one in the same.

Mags' truck rumbled to a stop in front of a two-story brick house. She climbed out and sniffed the air. "Lilac and arachnid," she concluded. Both were nearby. She retrieved a shop vac and some industrial pesticides and went up to the porch.

"Oh. Thank. God," Evan Constantine said as he yanked the door open. "They're everywhere." He fitfully pulled at his bowtie as he stepped aside to usher Mags into the house.

"The basement," Evan said. "I don't think one of 'em bit me, but I mean, it's only been a little bit."

"Recluse spider bite symptoms don't show up right away," Mags said, opening the basement door and shining a flashlight on the wooden steps. "And it's pretty rare for them to bite anyway."

"Recluse?" Evan said. "How do you know it's, uh, that kind of spider."

Mags turned slowly to her client and grinned. "I just know."

Mags marched down the stairs and turned on the overhead light at the bottom. "A little redness. Smaller chance of nausea and chills." She smirked. "Typical Saturday morning after a Friday night out, am I right?"

"Uh," Evan said.

"Well, except for the possible seizures and coma."

"What?"

"Don't worry," Mags said. "You probably don't have recluse spiders." She looked around at the room packed full of crates and things covered with tarps. A playground for the shy little recluse spiders and who knows what else. There could be all sorts of creepy crap hiding in there.

Well, this could be interesting.

"Mr. Constantine," Mags said. "You go on upstairs. What you probably have here is the common American house spider. Or maybe a wolf spider. Nothing to worry about."

"Great. Well, good luck with that." Evan bolted up the stairs.

The light flickered.

Mags spotted some webs right away. Recluse spiders are hunters. They spin webs, but they're usually down low, more for show than for catching prey. These webs? They were up high; intricate patterns.

Mags moved further into the basement, pushing aside storage crates and old exercise equipment. She found and cleaned up a few egg sacks, but these were garden-variety house spider eggs. The deeper she moved into the basement, though, the more complicated the webs became.

"Geez, doesn't that guy ever clean down here?" she muttered.

The basement seemed to go on and on. Like the dimensions down here were different than for the main level of the house. The webs started to connect more back here, eventually forming elaborate artistic renderings of forests and alien worlds and, in a far corner full of shelves with 1980s teen sex comedies, she spotted…a house?

Mags sighed. She'd seen this once before. It was during a very strange chapter in her pest control life; the story of which she reserved for late nights, several whiskies deep with the other exterminators. For them, their strangest experiences usually involved unexpected snakes in sock drawers that have things in them very different than socks, or customers answering the door naked.

Mags, though, she knew there were weirder things out there.

"Come out, please," Mags said as she stood at what might be the entrance to the web house.

"Dang it," a defeated voice said from within.

Six doleful eyes peered at Mags as the six-foot spider lumbered out of its web house and stood before her. The violin-shaped front half of its body shuddered nervously.

Mags brandished the hose from the shop vac as if that could do anything against a spider this size.

"An ultimate recluse spider," Mags said. "The artwork

was a dead giveaway."

The spider shrugged all its shoulders.

"You know you gotta go," Mags said.

The spider nodded sadly, but didn't move.

"Don't make me get rough," Mags said. She was a champion all-creatures wrestler, but she didn't like to play that card too often. She'd been off the circuit for years. There were still a number of zoos she was banned from.

"Everything okay down there?" Evan called.

"Yes," Mags called.

"No," the spider called.

"What?" Evan said.

"Just trying to decide between Hardbodies II and Meatballs III," Mags said.

"Um, okay…" Evan said. He went back upstairs to check on his soufflé.

"Spider, you gotta go," Mags said.

"Scared," the spider said.

"You can't hide down here forever like a…well, like a recluse, spider."

"Where would I go?" the spider asked.

"Anywhere but my client's house," Mags said.

The spider looked around helplessly.

Mags scanned the 80s video shelf. Sandwiched between "Losin' It" and Police Academy VHS tapes was a stapled dot matrix script for the 1985 Spider-Man movie that was commissioned, but never produced. "Know who this is?" Mags asked, showing the spider the red body-suited man on the cover.

"Spiderman?" the recluse spider said.

"That's right," Mags said. "It's not Hornet-man or Horse-fly Man. It's SPIDER-MAN. Know why? Because spiders are fierce and brave. They don't hide in basements surrounded by thigh-masters and boob movies. You can do this, spider."

"I can do this," the spider repeated.

"You're a fighter, not a hider."

"Can I bite people?"

"I wish you wouldn't," Mag said. "But you do you."

"Where will I go?"

"There are some lovely barns just begging for a reenactment of 'Charlotte's Web,'" Mags said.

"Well…" the spider said.

"Otherwise…you know." Mags held up the vacuum hose. The spider, thankfully, had very little understanding of the practical reality that there was no way to suck up a spider her size with a hose that size.

"All right then," the spider said. "I am brave. I can do this."

"Go see the world, my reclusive spider friend," Mags called and waved.

The spider waddled up the stairs, out of Evan Constantine's house. She attempted to start a new life in a barn…where she was promptly swatted by a farmer with good aim and the Sunday New York Times.

Evan and Mags kicked back with popcorn and the 1984 classic "Hot Dog…the Movie".

Inspired by ATARI BYTES episode 202: SPIDER FIGHTER.

LIFE IN THREE PARTS

Nicole Sanchez was seventeen when the movie "Galaxy Beyond" came out. The trailer looked amazing. The special effects! Robots! Space battles! And the pilot of the lead ship – the StarCrusher – was kind of hot. Nicole stood in line for hours with her friends Mia, Quentin, Julia and Steve for hours to get tickets. They sang songs. They had dance-offs. The waiting for the movie part was almost better than the watching the movie part.

Almost.

Sitting there in the dark watching this epic battle for galactic peace unfurl, Nicole had never been happier.

"That was a-may-zing," Nicole told her friends through a mouthful of popcorn as they left the theater.

"*Pew pew*," Mia said, simulating the sleek Level One Laser Fighters soaring past the evil Robot Vanguard's enemy lines.

Quentin and Julia recreated movie heroes' Dax and Sharona's witty banter: "I saw you looking at me." "I wasn't looking at you, I was just daydreaming about a Klondorian Swamp Spider landing on your head."

Steve was…less impressed. "Cheap special effects. Wooden dialogue. Cal Fusterian might be a decent enough director, but he's a lousy scriptwriter."

The movie took off. Toys and games soon followed. Nicole wasn't shy about being a teenager who loved her Galaxy Beyond bedsheets and footie pajamas. "Dax is on my butt," she told Mia. "What's not to love?'

It wasn't long before official word came down there would be a sequel: "Galaxy Beyond: Vanguard Vengeance".

A collective "yay!" from the group.

The movie will be out in three years.

Oh.

*****

After graduation, Nicole and Mia roomed together at State U. Steve rushed a fraternity at the school. Julia attended a drama school upstate and Quentin took a job at his dad's construction company to save up money.

Between "Galaxy Beyond" films, the actress who played Sharona won an academy award for playing the sister of a cancer survivor. And the actor who played Dax got a DUI conviction and starred in a mediocre western during a brief western movie fad.

When the "Vanguard Vengeance" release date was announced, Nicole and Mia asked Steve if he wanted to go to opening night. But the frat was hosting a "Mix-Master Mixer", whatever that is, that night and Steve was on ladle duty, so he couldn't go.

Julia wanted to go, but she was starring in an all-female stage production of a Three Stooges bio called "Three Bitches". Julia was playing Curly.

Quentin drove up from the old hometown. "Here we are again," he said as they stood in the theater lobby. "I like the old theater better."

Mia nodded. "Yeah, this is a sterile multiplex. Not like our old movie house."

"Probably no bats in the balcony, though," Nicole pointed out.

"Galaxy Beyond: Vanguard Vengeance" was…pretty good. Dax and Sharona were on point. Most of the new characters were fun, except maybe the floating, disembodied android head that kept singing opera. The plot was, well, a little thin, more of a bridge between part one of the trilogy and the inevitable part three. Having the Klondorian Swamp Spider turn out to hold the literal key to the Vault of Knowledge, was shocking, but less so than the spider's death bed confession of his shared ancestry with Dax.

The three friends jabbered a while in the lobby afterwards. "Want to get a beer?" Nicole asked.

"Nah, I gotta head back," Quentin said. "We're laying the foundation on a plasma donation center tomorrow."

"*Pew-pew*," Mia said.

"Not that kind of plasma."

"Oh. Well, okay," Nicole said, sorry her old friend had to bail so soon.

"Next time, maybe," Quentin said. "Thanks for the movie." Then he left, never to return.

*****

Three years plus a summer later, "Galaxy Beyond III: Closure" opened just in time for the holiday movie-going crowd. Blue, fuzzy wallaby-looking creatures with multiple horns on their heads filled the toy stores. These "Werbils", were the new creature from this installment of the movie.

Grad student Nicole called Mia to see if they could go. "One last opening night. Round out the trilogy," she said…

…to Mia's voice mail.

By the time Mia called back, the movie premiere had passed. "Brad and I were in Vancouver. It was epic."

Because of schedules and hot ticket sales, Nicole didn't get to see "Closure" until it had already been out three weeks. Avoiding spoilers was hard, but worth it. Nicole wept like a teenage her when Dax succumbed to the wounds inflicted by the Dark Duke, the big bad who arose in part two and seemed poised to rule the galaxy in part three only to be defeated by Sharona and her harp-knife. It was Dax who created the distraction that gave Sharona time to carry out her galaxy-saving plan. But at such a cost!

Even as the lights came up after the end credits, Nicole was still pulling herself together. Alone. Quentin, Steve, Julia, even Mia. No one cared anymore, it seemed.

*****

Like the StarCrusher hurtling through the journey-warp, time passed quickly. Twenty years later, the Internet buzzed with the news that Galaxy Beyond was being rebooted. Or revived? One or the other. The actress who played Sharona, now a multi-award winner, had been handed a buttload of cash to reprise her role, though it was rumored she would die perhaps as soon as the first movie in this new trilogy.

Nicole considered not going. She'd left the galaxy beyond a long time ago. And the friends that were an important part of it. She'd had a falling out with Julia over some stupid political thing. Quentin died in a car wreck about five years after the last movie.

But what about Steve and Mia? Should Nicole hit them up on social media?

"Nah," Nicole muttered. "Maybe 'Galaxy Beyond' is just for me know."

But she didn't really believe it.

Nicole was living in the old hometown again, having taken a position with a graphic design firm there. It seemed right to see the launch of a new "Galaxy Beyond" trilogy in the same theater the old trilogy launched in.

As she sat with her popcorn and chocolate-based confection waiting for the movie to start, a voice said, "This seat taken." Without even looking up, she answered. "Of course not, Steve."

Steve plopped into the seat and helped himself to some of Nicole's popcorn. He was going grey already, but he was still as much of a mooch as always.

"Uh, so, can I sit here?" Julia said, a little awkwardly, from the aisle.

Nicole gave a half smile. "Well, the 'Galaxy Beyond' galactic Congress has room for all types, so why not this theater? Yeah, sit down, goofball." Whatever they had been fighting about melted like the fake butter on the popcorn.

"Save a space for me," Mia said.

" 'bout time," Nicole said. "The others made their entrances already."

Was the ending predictable and fan-servicey? Absolutely. And so was the film up on the screen: "Galaxy Beyond: Renewal".

And Nicole loved all of it.

Inspired by ATARI BYTES episode 203: STAR WARS: THE RETURN OF THE JEDI – DEATH STAR BATTLE

TINY TIM'S ATARI DREAMS

That Christmas morn faded into milky twilight. The songs had all been sung. The mulled wine drunk. The turkey carcass was no longer big as the lad who fetched it for Scrooge; diminished in celebration of the day by the Cratchet family.

Scrooge slipped away into the night, floating on a cloud of newfound humanity. He finished out the day enjoying a Christmas cordial with his nephew Fred.

Then home to a restful sleep free of spirits.

The next morning Scrooge invited his bewildered and much put-upon assistant Bob Cratchet to discuss the terms of his employment over a bowl of hot punch.

Things were glorious in that new era.

For about a week.

One morning just after the new year, Bob Cratchet came into the offices of Scrooge and Marley. For once, he was the one wearing the dour expression.

"Bob Cratchet, my boy," Scrooge's voice boomed from across the room, He had been carefully attending to the new stove providing heat to the offices. "Greetings."

"Mr. Scrooge, sir," Bob Cratchet began, pausing – procrastinating really – by hanging his threadbare wool coat and hat upon the hook. "You've been so kind to my family these last few days, sir. Tiny Tim is much the stronger for it. I shudder to burden you further."

Scrooge chuckled. It still sounded a bit strange – more

wheeze than mirth, but he was working on it. "Nonsense," he said, good-naturedly. "I have a great many years of disservice to repay. How may I help?"

"Well, you see, sir," Cratchet said, "It's Tiny Tim, sir." Without even realizing, he took the poker from Mr. Scrooge and stirred the coals in the fire.

"Oh, dear," Scrooge said. "The boy hasn't taken a turn, has he?"

"No, sir," Cratchet said. "Quite the opposite."

"Whatever do you mean, my boy?"

"Well, sir," Cratchet began, searching clumsily for words. "He's more energetic than ever. Doesn't tire as easily – and we thank the good lord for that to be sure – but, well, he's bored, sir."

A flicker of indignation sputtered in the cold recesses of Scrooge's once dark heart. *Bored*? Are there no trades he could apprentice to? What of schooling? Put him to work mining the coal Cratchet is so fond of. What right did lame boys like Tim have to complain of boredom?

But that was the old Scrooge; the compassionless Scrooge. The new Scrooge said instead, "Perhaps your young man needs a hobby." The grin was not completely forced, but it was a little forced; gold tooth glinting in the firelight. "What are the young man's interests?"

Cratchet shifted in his seat, warming to the fire and the direction of this awkward conversation. "Well, he has dreams, sir. Fantastic, amazing dreams. Spaceships and exotic lands. Explorers and monsters and ghosts."

"Ghosts!" Scrooge shouted.

"Yes, sir, He says these ghosts live in a maze and chase people around, gobbling little marbles. Oh, it's all the stuff of a boy's wild imagination."

"Good heavens," Scrooge said.

"But, my boy," Cratchet said, "he's never been able to run and jump like the other boys, Mr. Scrooge. He's beginning to taste what that might be like – all thanks to your generosity, I might add – and well, he has the impatience of youth. You remember what it's like, sir."

Scrooge cast his mind back to the dour rigidity of his

own youth when education and study snuffed the light out of imagination. "Imagination," he heard himself mutter. "The frivolity of youth is…"

His contemptuous rant was cut short by the thought of those spirits and all they had shown him. Standing in his old school room, watching young Scrooge sitting alone working on his sums while everyone else went home to their families.

Bob Cratchet looked at his employer. His impulse was to flinch, of course, but the look on Scrooge's face – eyes still dark, but less so. There was more color in the cheeks and thin lips cracked into a half smile.

"My boy," Scrooge said. "I have a plan…"

Hours later, a tense Ebenezer Scrooge made his way along the docks. It was dirty, cold, smelled of rotten fish. Scrooge didn't belong here, would never have come here in his former guise. Yet, he knew exactly where he was. Thank you, Spirit of Christmas Yet to Come.

Old Joe was ensconced under the bridge; his thick, massive frame nearly indistinguishable from the piles holding up the bridge. Like a crocodile, Old Joe's eyes cut through the darkness and followed Scrooge for a long while before he spoke.

"A quid for the coat, guvenor," Old Joe said. "And I'd be doing a favor taking that hat off your hands for no more than the effort to lift it."

Scrooge tried to tamp down the queasy look on his face. "Old Joe, I presume?" he said.

"Your servant, sir," Old Joe growled.

"I require your services," Scrooge said.

"Do tell," Old Joe said, amused. "You don't look like one to consort with the…other folk."

"Nonetheless," Scrooge said. "I am in need of entertainments."

Old Joe smirked. "You've come to the wrong docks for that."

"Fool," Scrooge said. "I seek toys. Games. Amusements for a young boy."

Old Joe chuckled and reached languidly to one side. He produced from a sack: marbles, checkers, conkers, spinning tops, and a …hobby horse?

Scrooge bought them all – at prices naturally inflated to compensate Old Joe for his exertions; prices that at any level represented more than Scrooge had paid for anything in his entire, miserly life.

At the tiny home of the Cratchet family, Tiny Tim wore the flush of renewed hope and vigor, not yet free of his crutch – thought that would come by the grace of God and Mr. Scrooge's investments in his welfare – but he was also feeling a bit mopey.

"Come now and help with this bit of maths," Peter encouraged, for Tim was a whiz at mathematics, despite his young age. "If I'm to be apprenticed to a businessman, I've got to be able to get my sums right."

"Maybe later," Tiny Tim said.

"Tim, dear, there is still a bit of figge pudding left," his mother said. "Care for a bowl?"

"No thank you, mother," Tim said. Though he already slouched a bit, he seemed to sink further into the hearth by which he warmed himself.

A knock at the door and Mr. Scrooge was granted access, arms wide and loaded down with gifts. It was Christmas morning all over again; except, of course, it wasn't, as Tiny Tim's siblings soon learned to their bitter and, let's be honest, life-long resentment.

"My boy," Scrooge said once he'd piled his burden upon the table and regained his breath from his exertions. "Your father tells me you dream of adventure and faraway places." The words were a bit distasteful on Scrooge's tongue still, but he was working on it.

Tim brightened up. "Oh, yes, Mr. Scrooge! I would so dearly love to soar through outer space, battling monsters and the like. Or run through the jungle collecting treasures. I can picture it so well in my mind."

Peter scoffed. "Outer space? What nonsense."

"What's wrong with the space we have now?" his sisters chimed in, in eerie unison.

"Well, dear boy," Scrooge said, "in these bundles are the very things to spark a boy's sense of fun and adventure."

"For me?" Tim said.

"Certainly," Scrooge said. "All for you."

Tim wasted no time ripping open the parcels. Spilling forth were all manner of board games, playing cards, and intricate mechanical toys – pirates and clowns and monkeys that climbed ladders and such. The new-found optimist Scrooge had even purchased hoops and ropes for skipping in the hopes that Tim one day soon would have the strength to use them.

Peter was pretty jealous, but put on a supportive face.

Tim, though? Well, his ever-present smile faltered just a bit. "Oh," he said, dully and leaned back on his crutch.

"Is there a problem, dear?" his mother asked.

"Oh, no, Mother," Tim said. "These are lovely gifts, to be sure. Just not…what I had in mind."

"Tim," his mother reproached.

Scrooge held up a hand. "Let the boy speak."

And Tim did. "Well, these are...boring."

That's when Ebenezer Scrooge lost his figge pudding.

"Pardon me," he began. "Have you no refuge or resource? Are there no entertainments at hand? I help to stave off your listlessness at great expense. You can find...fun...if you open your eyes, child. Those who are without outlet for creativity must surely create it."

"But I cannot, Mr. Scrooge," Tim said. "I don't...feel like it."

"If you would rather be BORED," said Scrooge bitterly. "Then you'd better do it and decrease the surplus happiness."

With that, Scrooge stomped out of the tiny home of the Cratchet family, the few bits of artwork on the wall shuddered as the door slammed behind him.

Soot dirtied a fresh snowfall that crunched beneath Scrooge's well-worn boots. "Of all the ungrateful..." he started, reluctant to finish the thought, lest he betray his new persona.

Unsure what to do now, Scrooge kept walking, head bowed, avoiding all he passed, as per his custom, but for different reasons now. Old Scrooge was sad and angry, but he understood how to do that. He didn't know how to be happy, generous Scrooge yet. It was confusing. Scrooge didn't like confusing. He liked black and white. The child, Tim, added shades of color to his typical monochrome pallet and it was discomfiting.

So lost in his thoughts he was that Scrooge would have topped out on collision with the specter before him. But as it was a specter, he passed right through; only vaguely aware something had happened; the way you might register something in your peripheral vision without seeing it fully.

"Ebenezer," a man's voice said as if speaking through water.

He knew right away what was happening.

"Not again, spirit," Scrooge groaned. "Leave me be."

The ghost spoke again. "Face me, man."

Scrooge, by this point, knew not to argue. He turned and looked into the round, cherubic face of a man seemingly much younger than himself. He wore oddly shaped spectacles and a shirt with no sleeves. The lettering on the shirt was a nonsense jumble of letters. A-T-A-R-I. His trousers were a strong, heavy, cotton fabric , which he'd heard rumor was becoming fashionable in France. "Denim, he sneered."

"What the f?" the spirit asked, then cleared its otherworldly throat. "Sorry. I meant 'Pardon?'"

"I've learned my lesson, spirit," Scrooge said. "Why do you haunt me yet again?

The spirit shrugged. "New day, new lesson," it said. "Look, I'm the spirit of Gaming Yet to Come."

"Gaming?" Scrooge said. "Oh, you mean because of this disagreeable exchange with Tiny Tim. Well, the boy just doesn't understand games, is all."

"Well," the spirit said. "He understands that those games you brought suck."

Scrooge frowned. "Suck?" he repeated. "Explain."

"Never mind," the spirit said. "Just watch."

Thick hands on jiggly biceps waved as the spirit of Gaming Yet to Come opened a starry portal between Scrooge and him. A hiss of steam and flash of light later and Scrooge held in his hands a black box with ornate, rounded, wood-grain trim. Six elaborately twisted levers extended from the top and thick pipes of shiny tin encircled the monstrosity.

"What the devil…" Scrooge began.

"Behold," the ghost of Gaming Yet to Come said, "the world's first Atari 2600 Steam Punk Heavy Sixer." The pride in the spirit's voice was unmistakable. He studied Scrooge for a moment, then handed the bewildered man a pair of goggles. "Here," he said. "You'll need these."

The spirit quickly explained to Scrooge how a steam punk video game console worked – "It runs on lamp oil," he explained. Scrooge understood not a word, but he was a smart man and memorized what he was told.

The spirit handed Scrooge two game cartridges;

Gatling Gun Command and *Industrial Revolution*.

"My time on this Earth grows short," the spirit said. "Little more than *Pole Position* time trials."

Scrooge didn't understand that either.

The spirit faded away.

Armed with the gifts the spirit had given him, Scrooge dazzled Tiny Tim with these bizarre new gifts. The boy, inexplicably, took to them like the ducks on the river he used to love watching so much. You know, when going outside was the only way to have fun.

The boy and his siblings whiled away the rest of that day lost in the oil-fueled adventures splayed before their eyes on one wall of the Cratchet home.

At one point, the wee boy was heard saying, "God bless us, everyone. But, Peter, if you beat my high score again, I'll show you the business end of my cane."

Inspired by ATARI BYTES episode 204, the Dickens tale "A Christmas Carol" and every Scrooge adaptation ever.

Go to www.carnivalofgleecreations.com for more information about William Allen Pepper's podcasts ATARI BYTES and IT'S A PODCAST, CHARLIE BROWN, as well as his books and other projects.

www.ingramcontent.com/pod-product-compliance
Lightning Source LLC
LaVergne TN
LVHW041622060526
838200LV00040B/1398